GITANJALI

Rabindranath
Tagore

吉檀迦利

[印度] 泰戈尔 著

[美] 马克·麦金尼斯 绘　　萧兴政 译

云南出版集团
云南人民出版社

果麦文化　出品

目 录

译序　　响自秘林的芦笛

泰戈尔的诗集《吉檀迦利》已经有几个中译本，影响之大，可以说进入了许多读者的血脉。为何还要增加新译本？请容我简要说明一下，顺便谈谈我对泰戈尔和《吉檀迦利》的理解。

我二十来岁时读了冰心的《吉檀迦利》译文，当时把它当成爱情诗来读，和许多人一样，我曾为泰戈尔诗作中的纯粹、虔诚、爱的情感所打动。八十年代末，在厦大读研时，为了追溯这位印度诗人诗意的源头，我查阅了许多印度文学资料，除了感受到印度诗文之美外，我还隐约感受到了印度古诗的虔诚、灵秘、善感和热烈。

2002 年，我无意间下载到泰戈尔自译的《吉檀迦利》英文文本，看了颇为感动，终于见到了庐山真面目。当时，我在厦门大学英文系任教已经七年多，一门心思用在教学与英文诗歌创作上，且在剑桥大学出版社的刊物上发表了英文诗作，可我并没有想要做诗歌翻译或写中文诗。2003 年，我读了一部有关泰戈尔评传的英文著作，*Rabindranath Tagore—The Myriad-Minded Man*，可译为《拉宾德拉纳特·泰戈尔——多才多艺的人》，看完之后，觉得国内读者对泰戈尔以及印度灵性了解不足，第一次产生了翻译《吉檀迦利》的想法。随着知识储备的增加和对文本认识的深入，我觉得有必要重新翻译这部作品。

2004 年 10 月，我带着极大的爱心、恭敬心开始翻译，尽我当时的中英文能力，半年内完成了译文初稿。译诗无需太多理论，只需译者一颗敏感的心，对原文本语言与目标文本语言的熟练把握，以及与原文作者心领神会，在信、雅、达的基础上，在灵性上与作者合拍，表达出诗集的精神内涵。

《吉檀迦利》孟加拉语原名为 *Gitanjali*，英文直译为 *Song Offerings*，中文直译为《献歌集》，以诗歌作为向“神”的献礼。许多诗篇中，抒情主人时时渴望与不可言说的“源”（或者神）交流和相融，我的译文突出了这一点。冰心在译著简短序言中提到《吉檀迦利》充满人爱温情，却很少提及神人相融的情感。泰戈尔诗篇中的“你”常常是神或终极圆满状态的拟人，梵、涅槃、道、自然之灵，甚至死神，一旦用“你”来表现，“我”就是那完整里的微尘，渴望回归。渴望皈依“神”、回归圆满是《吉檀迦利》的主旨。

我和泰戈尔、冰心做了一次超越时空的精神交流。冰心带着虔诚，倾尽全力翻译，我的新译本个别用词没法摆脱她的选择，比如“足音”“诸天”等。由于时代在变，行文用词习惯也在变，当时的语言现在读起来不够朗朗上口，有些词的词义发生了变化，有必要更新，比如，冰心译本中“工作”一词全文出现 13 次，多数地方指的是孟加拉地区的苦力活（work），我在译文中将其全部换掉。冰心译文之白璧微瑕，我有专文讨论，不在此细说。我还写了一篇题为《泰戈尔和 < 吉檀迦利 >》的长文作为附录，希望它有助于读者更客观地了解泰戈尔和欣赏这部诗集。

2004 年至今，十五年过去了，按我个人的经验，每过十年，今我可为故我师。此间，我创作了大量中英文诗歌，开设了“英文诗歌阅读与创作”课程，阅读了大量文学典籍和印度灵性方面的书籍，除了印度两大史诗《摩诃婆罗多》《罗摩衍那》，还有英文版的《印度哲学》。随着对英文诗歌以及对泰戈尔更深入的理解，我觉得自己的英文能力以及内心状态，使我能够跨越时空进入泰戈尔的内心世界，用中文唱出同样真纯的孟加拉曲调。

十五年来，我不断以新的眼光，无数次阅读、修改译文，对《吉檀迦利》的感觉，就像酒窖里的美酒，储藏越久越甘醇。

1913 年，泰戈尔因《吉檀迦利》获得诺贝尔文学奖，随后这部诗集感动了世界。初读泰戈尔诗歌，读者一定为之震撼，不仅中国读者，整个西方的大文豪、科学家、政治家和宗教人士等，包括叶芝、庞德、聂鲁达和爱因斯坦等人，无一不被它深深打动。叶芝曾在伦敦公交车上阅读《吉檀迦利》，默默流泪。

诗篇中表达的情感，包括对神无限的爱，与神分离的痛苦，万物一体的宇宙整体意识，对生命和自然的礼赞，对死亡的思考与超越，对至纯婴儿和母爱的赞美，对祖国的热爱，和对离世爱人的追思，等等，情感细腻、跌宕起伏、波澜壮阔、扣人心弦，令人叹为观止。

为何诗人有这样的表现力？我在印度灵性传统中寻找到了答案。印度是婆罗门教或印度教的故乡，也是耆那教、佛教和锡克教的故乡，可以说是人类灵性觉醒、繁花似锦的精神故乡。作为一个印度诗人，我想，泰戈尔感动西方的不仅仅是他的真诚和谐的英文语言，全新的散文体诗歌，更在于诗集字里行间传递的印度人的灵性与虔诚。泰戈尔说过："真正的文学是对生命的真诚，而不仅仅是辞藻。"

泰戈尔在演讲中曾多次强调他的信仰是诗人的信仰，他的神不只是印度灵性传统中的神。他绝对不会非此即彼，陷入宗教门派纷争，他的神又是道、涅槃、梵等终极之源的神格化。自然在他眼里是神的示现，所有树木花草、飞禽走兽都带有神的信息，与庄子"天地与我并生，而万物与我为一"的说法一致。许多篇章中，抒情主人与"你"那种相互渴望、水乳交融、相爱的狂喜，常常使读者将其当成表达人间至爱的爱情诗。

其实，这种向神奉爱的诗歌在印度源远流长。印度教十一世纪到十七世纪的虔信派运动（Bhakti Movement）是对宇宙维护神毗湿奴（Vishnu）的化身神克里希那（Krishna）的虔信和无限的爱，他吹着芦笛与无数虔诚的牧牛女起舞在秘林里，最主要的诗篇有《牧童歌》（*Gita Govinda*），与西方基督教《圣经》里《雅歌》表达的神爱、爱神的情感极其相似。《吉檀迦利》是印度奉爱诗歌（devotional poetry）传统的延续，使西方读者产生了强烈的共鸣。当然，泰戈尔曾经说："我的心灵是在一种自由的空气中成长起来的，不受任何教会信奉的经文的约束……我的宗教，完全是诗人的宗教。"他的敬拜是对创造和支撑万物存在之源的敬拜。

陷入物质主义的泥潭，忽视灵性，甚至连佛陀伟大的教导也被盖上一层迷信的尘灰，我们的心灵就无法舞蹈。当今中国人物质生活极为丰富，然而，许多人却并不幸福，不知道内心痛苦的根源何在。其实，这种痛苦来自与支撑个体生命的"源""道"或者"神"的分离。让我用水珠和大海做一个比喻，也许能得到打开诗人内心的钥匙。

假定水珠有类似人的自我意识，有维持自我个性和存在的强烈欲望。如果这个终极之源是大海，每个生命只是一滴水珠。然而，水珠获得个体性以后，就认定所有其他水珠以及生成它的大海都是"他者"，与自己没有本质的关联，那么，短暂存在，然后蒸发（死亡）就是它唯一的命运，尽管它维持自身存在和尽量表现自己的努力多么令人动容。相反，要是这滴水珠意识到自己的本质是H_2O，与大海同质，它的内在拥有大海所有的信息，存在形式可以变换，本质却永远不灭，这滴水珠与大海以及所有其他水珠就永远没有分离（即没有死亡）。

宇宙进化到了你出生的时刻，你从肉眼看不见的精子卵子而来，能量通过母亲的肉体形成你的身体。出生以后，脐带剪断，你马上有新的"脐带"，你通过呼吸、食物、皮肤接受阳光等方式与宇宙相关联。然而，一旦意识到个体性，你就忘记了这些，把支撑你的宇宙和生养你的母亲都当成“他者”，所有人和你都没有本质关联，自然中一切皆可为我所用。于是，你就在短暂的存在中尽量捣鼓，因为死亡是灭顶之灾。

其实，这种“分离”，只是你内心的幻象，你的肉体只是能量的物化，与树木花草没有什么不同，你那内在感知能力，或者说觉性，存在于众生之中，与道相连。万物其实都是你肉体的延伸，一切即我，我即一切。

《吉檀迦利》是一部充满丰富情感的诗集，可以把它理解为一部宗教抒情诗集，也可以理解为泰戈尔与内在神性的对话，甚至，也可以当成人间极致的爱情诗来读。泰戈尔是一个理想主义者，关心整个人类的命运，对人和自然充满无限温情，但他在现实生活中并非一帆风顺。他有挣扎、有痛苦，渴求内心的宁静。在《吉檀迦利》的 103 首诗中，有一个孤独、带有理想主义和贵族气质的泰戈尔，也有一个亲切的泰戈尔。在充满灵性、动荡不安的印度，他的生命体验与心灵独白，时隔一个世纪，日久弥新。相信任何年龄的读者，都能从泰戈尔的诗文中得到感动、启发，认识自我与自然万物的本质。希望在当今纷扰的生活中，泰戈尔的《吉檀迦利》能成为使我们心灵宁静的港湾。

新译文经过多年打磨修改，仍不免有疏漏之处，还请读者不吝指正。唯愿有缘的读者能更好地体会这部诗集的美与爱，从中得到心灵的滋养，不断体悟个体生命与“源”的关联，更多了解印度灵性，感悟道家和佛家的智慧。我深深地祝福你们，祝愿你们圆满幸福。我还要感谢朗诵爱好者萧雨淳先生认真朗读了我的译文，并对朗读不顺的地方提出修改意见。我的家人和好友，身边的和远方的，愿我们在念想中与天地合一。

萧兴政

厦门大学外文学院英文系

2019 年 4 月

吉檀迦利

1-103

GITANJALI

这易碎的陶杯，你一次次倒空，又不断充以新的生命。

Thou hast made me endless, such is thy pleasure. This frail vessel thou emptiest again and again, and fillest it ever with fresh life.

This little flute of a reed thou hast carried over hills and dales, and hast breathed through it melodies eternally new.

At the immortal touch of thy hands my little heart loses its limits in joy and gives birth to utterance ineffable.

Thy infinite gifts come to me only on these very small hands of mine. Ages pass, and still thou pourest, and still there is room to fill.

1

你已使我绵延无尽，这样做是你的快乐。这易碎的陶杯，你一次次倒空，又不断充以新的生命。

这小小的芦笛，你携带着它翻越山谷，用它吹奏常新的音乐。

在你双手神圣的爱抚下，我小小的心迷失在无边的喜悦中，发出难以言表的词调。

你无穷的赐予只注入我小小的手。时代过去了，你还在倾注，而我的手还有空处可供充满。

我的仰慕像一只快乐的鸟儿，振翅飞越海洋。

When thou commandest me to sing it seems that my heart would break with pride; and I look to thy face, and tears come to my eyes.

All that is harsh and dissonant in my life melts into one sweet harmony—and my adoration spreads wings like a glad bird on its flight across the sea.

I know thou takest pleasure in my singing. I know that only as a singer I come before thy presence.

I touch by the edge of the far-spreading wing of my song thy feet which I could never aspire to reach.

Drunk with the joy of singing I forget myself and call thee friend who art my lord.

2

当你命令我歌唱时，我的心似乎要因骄傲而胀裂；我仰望着你的脸，泪水涌上了眼眶。

我生命中所有烦躁和苦痛融化成一片甜美的和谐——我的仰慕像一只快乐的鸟儿，振翅飞越海洋。

我知道你喜悦我的歌唱。我知道只有作为一个歌者，我才能来到你面前。

我用我的歌曲远伸翅膀的末梢触及你的双脚，那是我从未奢望触及的。

在歌唱的欣喜中陶醉，我忘乎所以，你是我的主人，我却称你为朋友。

你音乐的圣川冲破一切冷漠的阻碍，向前奔流。

I know not how thou singest, my master! I ever listen in silent amazement.

The light of thy music illumines the world. The life breath of thy music runs from sky to sky. The holy stream of thy music breaks through all stony obstacles and rushes on.

My heart longs to join in thy song, but vainly struggles for a voice. I would speak, but speech breaks not into song, and I cry out baffled. Ah, thou hast made my heart captive in the endless meshes of thy music, my master!

3

我不知道你怎样歌唱，我的主人！我总在惊诧中静听。

你音乐的光芒照亮了世界。你音乐的生命气息弥漫了诸天。你音乐的圣川冲破一切冷漠的阻碍，向前奔流。

我的心渴望应和你的歌唱，却无奈挣扎不出一点声音。我想说话，但言语迸发不出歌声，我语不成声地叫喊。啊，你已把我的心囚禁在你音乐的漫天大网中，我的主人！

我要不断努力驱除心中一切邪恶，让我的爱之花常开。

Life of my life, I shall ever try to keep my body pure, knowing that thy living touch is upon all my limbs.

I shall ever try to keep all untruths out from my thoughts, knowing that thou art that truth which has kindled the light of reason in my mind.

I shall ever try to drive all evils away from my heart and keep my love in flower, knowing that thou hast thy seat in the inmost shrine of my heart.

And it shall be my endeavour to reveal thee in my actions, knowing it is thy power gives me strength to act.

4

我生命中的生命，我要不断努力保持身体洁净，因为我知道你生之爱抚正触及我的四肢。

我要不断努力使思想远离虚伪，因为我知道你是那点燃我心中理性之火的真理。

我要不断努力驱除心中一切邪恶，让我的爱之花常开，因为我知道，你已在我内心圣殿深处安放了座位。

我要竭力在我的行为中展现你，因为我知道，是你的神力给了我行动的力量。

今天，夏日来到我窗前，叹息低语；
蜂儿在花丛的宫殿里，尽情吟唱。

I ask for a moment's indulgence to sit by thy side. The works that I have in hand I will finish afterwards.

Away from the sight of thy face my heart knows no rest nor respite, and my work becomes an endless toil in a shoreless sea of toil.

Today the summer has come at my window with its sighs and murmurs; and the bees are plying their minstrelsy at the court of the flowering grove.

Now it is time to sit quiet, face to face with thee, and to sing dedication of live in this silent and overflowing leisure.

5

请容许我放任片刻，坐在你身旁。我手头的活儿稍后再做。

见不到你的脸孔，我的心既不知道安宁，也得不到歇息，我的劳作就变成无边苦力之海的无尽苦力。

今天，夏日来到我窗前，叹息低语；蜂儿在花丛的宫殿里，尽情吟唱。

现在，该静坐了，与你相对，在这静寂和充裕的闲暇里唱出生命的献歌。

虽然它颜色不艳，香气不浓，就用这朵花来做朝拜，趁时辰未过，采下它吧。

Pluck this little flower and take it, delay not! I fear lest it droop and drop into the dust.

It may not find a place in thy garland, but honour it with a touch of pain from thy hand and pluck it. I fear lest the day end before I am aware, and the time of offering go by.

Though its colour be not deep and its smell be faint, use this flower in thy service and pluck it while there is time.

6

摘下这朵小花，拿去吧，不要迟延！我怕它会枯萎，掉在尘土里。

也许它不配点缀你的花环，请你采下它，用你的手带来痛苦的一触荣耀它吧。我生怕在不知不觉中，白昼消残，过了献礼的时辰。

虽然它颜色不艳，香气不浓，就用这朵花来做朝拜，趁时辰未过，采下它吧。

就让我把生命变得单纯而正直，像一支芦笛。

My song has put off her adornments. She has no pride of dress and decoration. Ornaments would mar our union; they would come between thee and me; their jingling would drown thy whispers.

My poet's vanity dies in shame before thy sight. O master poet, I have sat down at thy feet. Only let me make my life simple and straight, like a flute of reed for thee to fill with music.

7

我的歌曲已卸去她的妆饰。她不再为衣饰感到骄傲。妆饰会阻碍我们的融合；它们会横阻在你我之间，它们叮铃铃的响声会淹没你的低语。

我诗人的虚荣在你面前羞惭地退去。啊，诗者之师，我已坐在你的脚前。就让我把生命变得单纯而正直，像一支芦笛，用你的音乐来充满。

唯恐衣饰受磨损，染上尘土，他不敢走进这世界。

The child who is decked with prince's robes and who has jewelled chains round his neck loses all pleasure in his play; his dress hampers him at every step.

In fear that it may be frayed, or stained with dust he keeps himself from the world, and is afraid even to move.

Mother, it is no gain, thy bondage of finery, if it keeps one shut off from the healthful dust of the earth, if it rob one of the right of entrance to the great fair of common human life.

8

那穿着王子般的衣袍，挂着珠宝项链的孩子，在玩耍中失去一切快乐；衣着羁绊他的每一步。

唯恐衣饰受磨损，染上尘土，他不敢走进这世界，甚至寸步不敢移动。

母亲，如果你用盛装艳服的束缚，使人远离大地健康的尘土，夺去一个人进入普通人生命盛大集会的权利，这是徒劳无功的。

你的欲望用它的气息触及灯火，灯火就顷刻熄灭。

O Fool, to try to carry thyself upon thy own shoulders! O beggar, to come beg at thy own door!

Leave all thy burdens on his hands who can bear all, and never look behind in regret.

Thy desire at once puts out the light from the lamp it touches with its breath. It is unholy—take not thy gifts through its unclean hands. Accept only what is offered by sacred love.

9

啊，傻子，竟然想把自己扛在肩上！啊，乞儿，竟然来到自家的门前乞讨！

把你的重负卸在他的手中吧，他能承受一切，而且永不为后悔而反顾。

你的欲望用它的气息触及灯火，灯火就顷刻熄灭。它是邪恶的——不要从它不洁的手中接受礼物。只领受神圣爱的赐予吧。

你歇足在最贫困，最低贱，最迷惘的人群中。

Here is thy footstool and there rest thy feet where live the poorest, and lowliest, and lost.

When I try to bow to thee, my obeisance cannot reach down to the depth where thy feet rest among the poorest, and lowliest, and lost.

Pride can never approach to where thou walkest in the clothes of the humble among the poorest, and lowliest,and lost.

My heart can never find its way to where thou keepest company with the companionless among the poorest, the lowliest, and the lost.

10

这是你的脚凳，你歇足在最贫困，最低贱，最迷惘的人群中。

我向你躬身敬礼，可我的敬意达不到你歇足的深处，那最贫困，最低贱，最迷惘的人群中。

傲慢永远抵达不了你身着粗服行走的地方，那最贫困，最低贱，最迷惘的人群中。

你与无人做伴者为伍，我的心永远找不到那个地方，那最贫困，最低贱，最迷惘的人群中。

他和耕作贫瘠土地的农夫在一起，和碎石造路的劳工在一起。

Leave this chanting and singing and telling of beads! Whom dost thou worship in this lonely dark corner of a temple with doors all shut? Open thine eyes and see thy God is not before thee!

He is there where the tiller is tilling the hard ground and where the pathmaker is breaking stones. He is with them in sun and in shower, and his garment is covered with dust. Put of thy holy mantle and even like him come down on the dusty soil!

Deliverance? Where is this deliverance to be found? Our master himself has joyfully taken upon him the bonds of creation; he is bound with us all for ever.

Come out of thy meditations and leave aside thy flowers and incense! What harm is there if thy clothes become tattered and stained? Meet him and stand by him in toil and in sweat of thy brow.

11

把颂唱和念珠撇下吧！在门窗紧闭、黑暗孤寂的圣殿一隅，你在敬拜谁呢？睁眼看看吧，你的上主不在你面前！

他和耕作贫瘠土地的农夫在一起，和碎石造路的劳工在一起。日晒雨打，他仍在他们当中，衣着蒙上尘土。脱下你的僧衣，甚至像他一样，下驾到尘土飞扬的土地吧！

解脱？哪里能找到那种解脱？我们的主已欣然把造物的锁链戴起；他和我们大家永远紧系在一起。

走出你的静坐冥想吧，丢开你的供花和供香！你的衣着变得褴褛和肮脏又有何妨？到他那里，站在他身边，和他一起劳累，汗流满面吧。

天刚破晓，我就驱车远行，穿越大千世界的旷野，在许多星体上留下辙痕。

The time that my journey takes is long and the way of it long.

I came out on the chariot of the first gleam of light, and pursued my voyage through the wildernesses of worlds leaving my track on many a star and planet.

It is the most distant course that comes nearest to thyself, and that training is the most intricate which leads to the utter simplicity of a tune.

The traveller has to knock at every alien door to come to his own, and one has to wander through all the outer worlds to reach the innermost shrine at the end.

My eyes strayed far and wide before I shut them and said "Here art thou!"

The question and the cry "Oh, where?" melt into tears of a thousand streams and deluge the world with the flood of the assurance "I am!"

12

我的旅程费时很长，旅途漫漫。

天刚破晓，我就驱车远行，穿越大千世界的旷野，在许多星体上留下辙痕。

去离你自己最近的地方，旅途最长；弹奏至纯的曲调，需要最繁琐的练习。

旅人要敲遍异乡人的门，才能最后来到自家的门前；人要在异域四处漂泊，才能最终到达最深的内殿。

我必先放眼四方，然后才能合上双眼说：“原来你在这里啊！”

那质问和呐喊“啊，在哪儿？”融化在千条泪河里，和“我在这儿！”坚定回答的洪流，一同泛滥了全世界。

我要唱的歌曲至今还未唱出。花儿尚未开放；只有风儿叹息而过。

The song that I came to sing remains unsung to this day.

I have spent my days in stringing and in unstringing my instrument.

The time has not come true, the words have not been rightly set; only there is the agony of wishing in my heart.

The blossom has not opened; only the wind is sighing by.

I have not seen his face, nor have I listened to his voice; only I have heard his gentle footsteps from the road before my house.

The livelong day has passed in spreading his seat on the floor; but the lamp has not been lit and I cannot ask him into my house.

I live in the hope of meeting with him; but this meeting is not yet.

13

我要唱的歌曲至今还未唱出。

这些日子我总在调理琴弦。

歌唱的时刻还未到来，歌词尚未填好，心中只有想望的痛苦。

花儿尚未开放；只有风儿叹息而过。

我未曾与他谋面，也不曾听过他的声音；我只听到他轻缓的足音从我屋前的路上传来。

整整一天，我消磨在地板上为他铺设座位；可是灯还未点上，我不能请他进屋。

我活在与他相会的期望中，但这相会，尚未到来。

我不曾问，你就给了我——这天空、光明，这躯体、生命与心灵。

My desires are many and my cry is pitiful, but ever didst thou save me by hard refusals; and this strong mercy has been wrought into my life through and through.

Day by day thou art making me worthy of the simple, great gifts that thou gavest to me unasked—this sky and the light, this body and the life and the mind—saving me from perils of overmuch desire.

There are times when I languidly linger and times when I awaken and hurry in search of my goal; but cruelly thou hidest thyself from before me.

Day by day thou art making me worthy of thy full acceptance by refusing me ever and anon, saving me from perils of weak, uncertain desire.

14

我欲念很多，我的哀求令人怜悯，可你从来都用断然的拒绝来拯救我；这坚定的慈悲已彻底被打造在我的生命中。

一天天，你使我更配得上领受那单纯而伟大的赐予，我不曾问，你就给了我——这天空、光明，这躯体、生命与心灵——拯救我脱离欲念过多的危险。

有时我无精打采地拖延，有时我醒悟，急忙寻找我的目标；你却在我面前狠心地隐藏起你自己。

通过时时拒绝我，一天天你使我更配得上你完全的接纳，把我从软弱、无常欲念的危险中拯救出来。

在晨光中，当金色的竖琴调好时，荣耀我，召我上前吧。

I am here to sing thee songs. In this hall of thine I have a corner seat.

In thy world I have no work to do; my useless life can only break out in tunes without a purpose.

When the hour strikes for thy silent worship at the dark temple of midnight, command me, my master, to stand before thee to sing.

When in the morning air the golden harp is tuned, honour me, commanding my presence.

15

我来到这儿为你歌唱。我的座位在你厅堂的一角。

在你的世界里，我无事可做；我无用的生命只能爆发出无目的的曲调。

在夜半黑暗的圣殿里，当静默敬拜你的钟声敲起时，召我站在你的面前歌唱吧，我的主人。

在晨光中，当金色的竖琴调好时，荣耀我，召我上前吧。

我应邀参加这世界的节庆，我的生命因此受到祝福。

I have had my invitation to this world's festival, and thus my life has been blessed. My eyes have seen and my ears have heard.

It was my part at this feast to play upon my instrument, and I have done all I could.

Now, I ask, has the time come at last when I may go in and see thy face and offer thee my silent salutation?

16

我应邀参加这世界的节庆，我的生命因此受到祝福。我听闻了许多，大开了眼界。

在这欢宴上，我要做的事是弹奏，我已倾尽了全力。

现在，我要问，让我进去景仰你的容颜，向你静默敬拜的时刻终于到来了吗?

我只在等候爱，最终要把自己托付在他的手里。

I am only waiting for love to give myself up at last into his hands. That is why it is so late and why I have been guilty of such omissions.

They come with their laws and their codes to bind me fast; but I evade them ever, for I am only waiting for love to give myself up at last into his hands.

People blame me and call me heedless; I doubt not they are right in their blame.

The market day is over and work is all done for the busy. Those who came to call me in vain have gone back in anger. I am only waiting for love to give myself up at last into his hands.

17

我只在等候爱，最终要把自己托付在他的手里。这是为何我如此迟延，为何一直为这个疏忽而内疚。

他们带着律法和习俗来紧紧束缚我；可我总是躲着他们，因为我只在等候爱，最终要把自己托付在他的手里。

人们责备我，说我冒失无礼；我也不怀疑他们的责备有道理。

集市日已过，忙碌的人都干完了活。那些徒劳来叫我的人都已含怒回去。我只在等候爱，最终要把自己托付在他的手里。

我不住地凝望远处阴沉的天空，我的心和不宁的风一道彷徨哀号。

Clouds heap upon clouds and it darkens. Ah, love, why dost thou let me wait outside at the door all alone?

In the busy moments of the noontide work I am with the crowd, but on this dark lonely day it is only for thee that I hope.

If thou showest me not thy face, if thou leavest me wholly aside, I know not how I am to pass these long, rainy hours.

I keep gazing on the far-away gloom of the sky, and my heart wanders wailing with the restless wind.

18

云霾堆积，黑暗笼罩。啊，爱人，为什么你让我在门外独自等候?

正午劳作繁忙时分，我在人群中，但在这黑暗、孤独的日子，只因为你，我才心存希望。

假如你不向我露面，倘若你撇开我完全不顾，我真不知道如何度过这漫长的雨天。

我不住地凝望远处阴沉的天空，我的心和不宁的风一道彷徨哀号。

从我的每一个鸟巢中，你的话语将展开歌声的翅膀。

If thou speakest not I will fill my heart with thy silence and endure it. I will keep still and wait like the night with starry vigil and its head bent low with patience.

The morning will surely come, the darkness will vanish, and thy voice pours down in golden streams breaking through the sky.

Then thy words will take wing in songs from every one of my birds' nests, and thy melodies will break forth in flowers in all my forest groves.

19

如果你静默不语，我就忍受着，用你的沉默充满我的心。我将静静地等候，像黑夜在星光灿烂中无眠，耐心低首。

清晨一定会到来，黑暗将要消隐，你声音的金色泉流将划破天空倾泻而下。

那时，从我的每一个鸟巢中，你的话语将展开歌声的翅膀，你悦耳的旋律将在我所有的林丛中绽放出花朵。

莲花盛开的那天，唉，我心魂飘荡却不自知。

On the day when the lotus bloomed, alas, my mind was straying, and I knew it not. My basket was empty and the flower remained unheeded.

Only now and again a sadness fell upon me, and I started up from my dream and felt a sweet trace of a strange fragrance in the south wind.

That vague sweetness made my heart ache with longing and it seemed to me that it was the eager breath of the summer seeking for its completion.

I knew not then that it was so near, that it was mine, and that this perfect sweetness had blossomed in the depth of my own heart.

20

莲花盛开的那天，唉，我心魂飘荡却不自知。我的花篮空空，花儿一直无人理睬。

只是时不时一阵忧愁袭来，我从梦中惊醒，感觉南风里有一股奇香的芳迹。

这朦胧的馨香使我渴望得心痛，我觉得这似乎是夏天热切的气息在寻求圆满。

我当时不知道它离我那么近，而且是我的，不知道这完美的馨香已在我自己的深心怒放。

潮水变得喧嚷，河岸上荫蔽的小径，
黄叶瑟瑟飘落。

I must launch out my boat. The languid hours pass by on the shore—Alas for me!

The spring has done its flowering and taken leave. And now with the burden of faded futile flowers I wait and linger.

The waves have become clamorous, and upon the bank in the shady lane the yellow leaves flutter and fall.

What emptiness do you gaze upon! Do you not feel a thrill passing through the air with the notes of the far-away song floating from the other shore?

21

我必须撑船出航。懒散的时光消逝在岸边——啊，我的光阴!

春天辞别了，它的花事已尽。如今带着无用落红的重负，我却等待、留连。

潮水变得喧嚷，河岸上荫蔽的小径，黄叶瑟瑟飘落。

你向虚空凝视什么！你没有感觉到空气中掠过一阵惊喜，带着飘自遥远彼岸歌声的音符吗?

我唯一的朋友，我最爱的人，我的家门是开着的——不要像梦一般地走过吧。

In the deep shadows of the rainy July, with secret steps, thou walkest, silent as night, eluding all watchers.

Today the morning has closed its eyes, heedless of the insistent calls of the loud east wind, and a thick veil has been drawn over the ever-wakeful blue sky.

The woodlands have hushed their songs, and doors are all shut at every house. Thou art the solitary wayfarer in this deserted street. Oh my only friend, my best beloved, the gates are open in my house—do not pass by like a dream.

22

在多雨七月的阴霾中，你行踪神秘，夜一般无声，躲过所有更夫。

今天，清晨闭上双眼，不理睬喧嚷东风的连连呼唤，一层厚厚的面纱遮蔽了永不入睡的碧空。

林地的歌声已沉寂，家家户户都关上了门。你是这冷寂街道上孤单的旅人。啊，我唯一的朋友，我最爱的人，我的家门是开着的——不要像梦一般地走过吧。

我今夜无眠，一次次我开门向黑暗中张望，我的朋友！

Art thou abroad on this stormy night on thy journey of love, my friend? The sky groans like one in despair.

I have no sleep tonight. Ever and again I open my door and look out on the darkness, my friend!

I can see nothing before me. I wonder where lies thy path!

By what dim shore of the ink-black river, by what far edge of the frowning forest, through what mazy depth of gloom art thou threading thy course to come to me, my friend?

23

在这暴风雨之夜，你还身在异乡，爱的旅途吗，我的朋友？天空像一个绝望者在哀号。

我今夜无眠，一次次我开门向黑暗中张望，我的朋友！

我看不见眼前的一切。我不知道你的道路是哪一条！

从什么漆黑河流朦胧的岸上，从什么远方愁眉不展的森林边缘，穿过什么昏暗迷离的深处，你摸索着来到我这里，我的朋友？

请你消除他的羞耻与匮乏，更新他的生命，就像把一朵花儿笼罩在你仁慈的夜幕下。

If the day is done, if birds sing no more, if the wind has flagged tired, then draw the veil of darkness thick upon me, even as thou hast wrapt the earth with the coverlet of sleep and tenderly closed the petals of the drooping lotus at dusk.

From the traveller, whose sack of provisions is empty before the voyage is ended, whose garment is torn and dust-laden, whose strength is exhausted, remove shame and poverty, and renew his life like a flower under the cover of thy kindly night.

24

假如白昼已逝，鸟儿不再歌唱，假如风儿已吹倦，那就用黑暗的帷幕把我严实地盖上吧，正如你在黄昏时用睡眠的衾被裹住大地，又温柔地合上睡莲的花瓣。

旅人的行程未尽，囊袋已空，行装破烂，尘土满身，精疲力竭，请你消除他的羞耻与匮乏，更新他的生命，就像把一朵花儿笼罩在你仁慈的夜幕下。

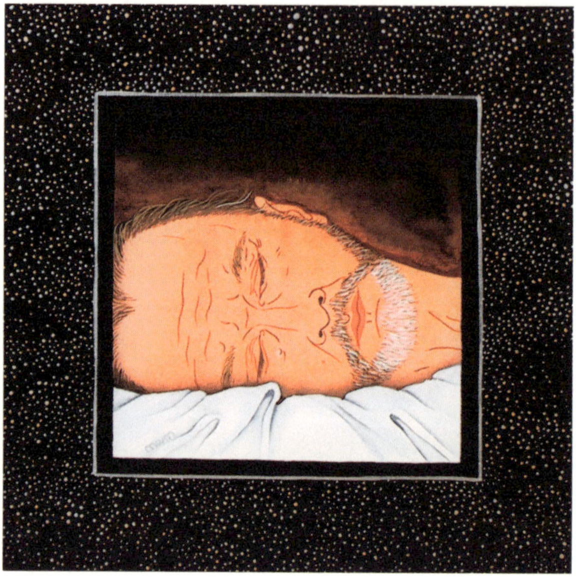

在这疲惫之夜，让我不做挣扎臣服于睡眠，全然地信靠你。

In the night of weariness let me give myself up to sleep without struggle, resting my trust upon thee.

Let me not force my flagging spirit into a poor preparation for thy worship.

It is thou who drawest the veil of night upon the tired eyes of the day to renew its sight in a fresher gladness of awakening.

25

在这疲惫之夜，让我不做挣扎臣服于睡眠，全然地信靠你。

让我不要强打我萎靡的精神，草率地准备对你的敬拜。

是你拉起夜的帷幕，盖上白日疲倦的眼睛，以使它醒来时在清新的喜悦中恢复眼力。

万籁俱寂的夜里，他来了，手持竖琴。

He came and sat by my side but I woke not. What a cursed sleep it was, O miserable me!

He came when the night was still; he had his harp in his hands, and my dreams became resonant with its melodies.

Alas, why are my nights all thus lost? Ah, why do I ever miss his sight whose breath touches my sleep?

26

他来了，就坐在我身边，我却没有醒来。多可恨的睡眠，唉，不幸的我啊！

万籁俱寂的夜里，他来了，手持竖琴，我的梦魂和他悦耳的旋律起了和鸣。

唉，为什么我夜夜就这样虚度？啊，他的气息触及我的睡眠，为何我还一直错过他？

一刹的闪电在我眼前拉下一幕更深的黑暗，我的心摸索着那夜的音乐召唤我的路径。

Light, oh where is the light? Kindle it with the burning fire of desire!

There is the lamp but never a flicker of a flame—is such thy fate, my heart? Ah, death were better by far for thee!

Misery knocks at thy door, and her message is that thy lord is wakeful, and he calls thee to the love-tryst through the darkness of night.

The sky is overcast with clouds and the rain is ceaseless. I know not what this is that stirs in me—I know not its meaning.

A moment's flash of lightning drags down a deeper gloom on my sight, and my heart gropes for the path to where the music of the night calls me.

Light, oh where is the light! Kindle it with the burning fire of desire! It thunders and the wind rushes screaming through the void. The night is black as a black stone. Let not the hours pass by in the dark. Kindle the lamp of love with thy life.

27

光明，哦，哪里有光明？用熊熊的热望之火燃起它吧！

有灯，却从未有一丝闪烁的火焰——这就是你的命运吗，我的心？啊，你远不如一死了之！

悲痛叩响你的门，她带来的音信是你的主还醒着，他召唤你穿过夜的黑暗，奔赴爱的幽会。

天空阴霾沉沉，雨下个不停。我不知道什么在我深心骚动——我不解其意。

一刹的闪电在我眼前拉下一幕更深的黑暗，我的心摸索着那夜的音乐召唤我的路径。

光明，哦，哪里有光明？用熊熊的热望之火燃起它吧！雷声轰鸣，狂风从天空咆哮而过。夜像黑岩一样黑。不要让光阴在黑暗中消逝。用你的生命燃起爱的灯火吧。

束缚是坚韧的，可要打破它们，我却心痛。我只要自由，可去期望它，我却感到羞耻。

Obstinate are the trammels, but my heart aches when I try to break them.

Freedom is all I want, but to hope for it I feel ashamed.

I am certain that priceless wealth is in thee, and that thou art my best friend, but I have not the heart to sweep away the tinsel that fills my room.

The shroud that covers me is a shroud of dust and death; I hate it, yet hug it in love.

My debts are large, my failures great, my shame secret and heavy; yet when I come to ask for my good, I quake in fear lest my prayer be granted.

28

束缚是坚韧的，可要打破它们，我却心痛。

我只要自由，可去期望它，我却感到羞耻。

我确知你身上有无价之宝，而且你是我的至交，可我不忍心清除我满屋的廉价之物。

我身上披着尘土和死亡之衣；我痛恨它，却又用爱拥抱它。

我债务缠身，失意潦倒，我的羞耻深重不可告人；可当我前来祈求福惠时，我又因惊恐而颤栗，生怕我的祈祷得到恩准。

当这道围墙一天天拔地而起时，在黑影中，我再也见不到真我。

He whom I enclose with my name is weeping in this dungeon. I am ever busy building this wall all around; and as this wall goes up into the sky day by day I lose sight of my true being in its dark shadow.

I take pride in this great wall, and I plaster it with dust and sand lest a least hole should be left in this name; and for all the care I take I lose sight of my true being.

29

我用我的声名围困的那个人在地牢中哭泣。我时刻不停地筑起围墙；当这道围墙一天天拔地而起时，在黑影中，我再也见不到真我。

我以这道高墙为荣，把它抹上沙土，唯恐在这声名上还留下一丝裂缝；只因我耗尽所有苦心，我再也见不到真我。

我独自出门赶赴幽会。可在寂静的黑暗中跟随我的人是谁呢？

I came out alone on my way to my tryst. But who is this that follows me in the silent dark?

I move aside to avoid his presence but I escape him not.

He makes the dust rise from the earth with his swagger; he adds his loud voice to every word that I utter.

He is my own little self, my lord, he knows no shame; but I am ashamed to come to thy door in his company.

30

我独自出门赶赴幽会。可在寂静的黑暗中跟随我的人是谁呢?

我走到一旁躲避他，可我摆脱不了他。

他大摇大摆，使地上尘土飞扬；我说的每一句话都掺杂着他的喧嚷。

他是我的小我，我的主，他不知道羞耻；和他结伴来到你门前，我感到羞愧。

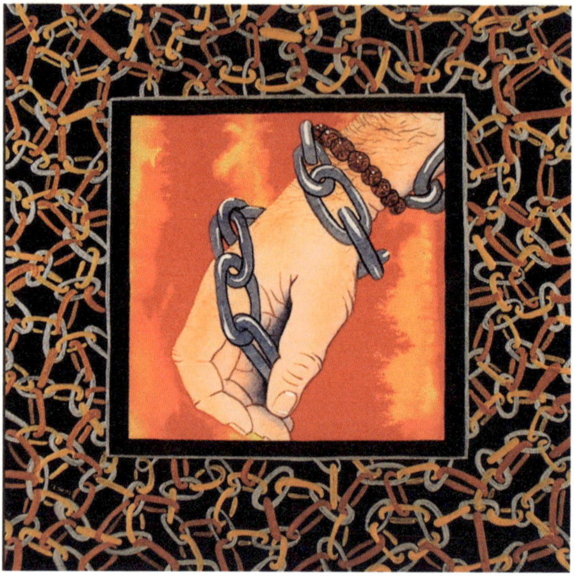

醒来时，我才发现我在自家的金库里做了囚徒。

"Prisoner, tell me, who was it that bound you?"

"It was my master," said the prisoner. "I thought I could outdo everybody in the world in wealth and power, and I amassed in my own treasure-house the money due to my king. When sleep overcame me I lay upon the bed that was for my lord, and on waking up I found I was a prisoner in my own treasure-house."

"Prisoner, tell me, who was it that wrought this unbreakable chain?"

"It was I," said the prisoner, "who forged this chain very carefully. I thought my invincible power would hold the world captive leaving me in a freedom undisturbed. Thus night and day I worked at the chain with huge fires and cruel hard strokes. When at last the work was done and the links were complete and unbreakable, I found that it held me in its grip."

31

“囚徒，告诉我，是谁把你绑起来的？”

“是我的主人，”囚徒说，“我本想我的财富与权力能胜过世上所有人，我把属于国王的钱财积聚在自家的金库里。当睡意袭来，我就躺到我主人的床上，醒来时，我才发现我在自家的金库里做了囚徒。”

“囚徒，告诉我，是谁锻造了这牢不可破的锁链？”

“是我，”囚徒说，“是我自己精心锻造的。我本想我无敌的权力会使世界臣服，使我有随心所欲的自由。因此，日日夜夜，我用烈火重锤打造这条铁链。终于完成了，链结妥当，牢不可破，我才发现它把我紧紧地锁住了。”

你的爱却不一样，比他们的爱伟大得多，你让我自由自在。

By all means they try to hold me secure who love me in this world. But it is otherwise with thy love which is greater than theirs, and thou keepest me free.

Lest I forget them they never venture to leave me alone. But day passes by after day and thou art not seen.

If I call not thee in my prayers, if I keep not thee in my heart, thy love for me still waits for my love.

32

世上爱我的人，想方设法稳稳地拉住我。你的爱却不一样，比他们的爱伟大得多，你让我自由自在。

他们从不敢对我撒手不管，以免我忘掉他们。日子一天天过去，而你从来不露面。

假如我不在祈祷中呼唤你，假如我不把你记在心上，你对我的爱仍在期待我的爱。

在黑夜里，我发现他们狂暴粗野地闯入我的圣堂，邪恶贪婪地攫取神坛上的祭品。

When it was day they came into my house and said, "We shall only take the smallest room here."

They said, "We shall help you in the worship of your God and humbly accept only our own share in his grace"; and then they took their seat in a corner and they sat quiet and meek.

But in the darkness of night I find they break into my sacred shrine, strong and turbulent, and snatch with unholy greed the offerings from God's altar.

33

白天的时候，他们来到我屋里说：“我们只占用最小的一间屋子。”

他们说：“我们要帮你敬拜你的上主，只谦卑地领受我们应得的一份恩典。”然后，他们就在屋角安静、谦卑地坐下。

但在黑夜里，我发现他们狂暴粗野地闯入我的圣堂，邪恶贪婪地攫取神坛上的祭品。

只要让我一息尚存，我就称你为我的一切。时刻把我的爱献给你。

Let only that little be left of me whereby I may name thee my all.

Let only that little be left of my will whereby I may feel thee on every side, and come to thee in everything, and offer to thee my love every moment.

Let only that little be left of me whereby I may never hide thee.

Let only that little of my fetters be left whereby I am bound with thy will, and thy purpose is carried out in my life—and that is the fetter of thy love.

34

只要让我一息尚存，我就称你为我的一切。

只要让我一念不灭，我就感觉你在我的周围，任何事我都请教你，时刻把我的爱献给你。

只要让我一息尚存，我就永远不会把你藏起来。

只要留给我镣铐的一小段，我就和你的意愿捆绑在一起，你的意旨就施行在我生命中——这镣铐就是你的爱。

在那里，心灵受你引领，走向不断开阔的思想与行为。

Where the mind is without fear and the head is held high;

Where knowledge is free;

Where the world has not been broken up into fragments by narrow domestic walls;

Where words come out from the depth of truth;

Where tireless striving stretches its arms towards perfection;

Where the clear stream of reason has not lost its way into the dreary desert sand of dead habit;

Where the mind is led forward by thee into ever-widening thought and action—

Into that heaven of freedom, my Father, let my country awake.

35

在那里，心没有恐惧，头高昂着；

在那里，知识免费；

在那里，世界没有被狭隘家国的围墙割裂成片断；

在那里，话说自真理深处；

在那里，不懈的努力张开臂膀追求完美；

在那里，理智的清流没有迷失在积习的荒漠中；

在那里，心灵受你引领，走向不断开阔的思想与行为——

进入那自由天国，我的父啊，让我的祖国觉醒吧。

请你根除，根除我心中的贫乏。赐给我力量，使我能轻松地承受喜悦与悲痛。

This is my prayer to thee, my lord—strike, strike at the root of penury in my heart.

Give me the strength lightly to bear my joys and sorrows.

Give me the strength to make my love fruitful in service.

Give me the strength never to disown the poor or bend my knees before insolent might.

Give me the strength to raise my mind high above daily trifles.

And give me the strength to surrender my strength to thy will with love.

36

这是我向你的祈祷，我的主——请你根除，根除我心中的贫乏。

赐给我力量，使我能轻松地承受喜悦与悲痛。

赐给我力量，使我的爱在奉献中果实累累。

赐给我力量，使我永不舍弃穷人，也永不向淫威屈膝。

赐给我力量，使我的心超越日常琐事。

再赐给我力量，使我心怀诚爱，让我的力量服从你的意志。

旧的辙痕刚刚依稀远去，新的疆域又奇妙地展开。

I thought that my voyage had come to its end at the last limit of my power—that the path before me was closed, that provisions were exhausted and the time come to take shelter in a silent obscurity.

But I find that thy will knows no end in me. And when old words die out on the tongue, new melodies break forth from the heart; and where the old tracks are lost, new country is revealed with its wonders.

37

精疲力竭时，我以为行程已尽——前路已绝，备粮耗尽，该在静谧朦胧中投宿了。

可我发现你的意志在我身上永无终了。旧的话语才到嘴边已成滥调，新的旋律又从心中迸发；旧的辙痕刚刚依稀远去，新的疆域又奇妙地展开。

日夜使我纷乱的种种欲念，本质上都是虚假和空洞。

That I want thee, only thee—let my heart repeat without end. All desires that distract me, day and night, are false and empty to the core.

As the night keeps hidden in its gloom the petition for light, even thus in the depth of my unconsciousness rings the cry—I want thee, only thee.

As the storm still seeks its end in peace when it strikes against peace with all its might, even thus my rebellion strikes against thy love and still its cry is—I want thee, only thee.

38

我要你，只要你——让我的心不停地兜念着。日夜使我纷乱的种种欲念，本质上都是虚假和空洞。

就像黑夜把对光明的祈求隐藏在朦胧里，我无意识的深处更是这样发出呼唤——我要你，只要你。

正如风暴竭尽全力撞击平静，仍然寻求终止于平静，我的反叛更是这样撞击着你的爱，它的呼唤仍然是——我要你，只要你。

当我的心冷酷干枯时，请为我降下慈悲的甘霖。

When the heart is hard and parched up, come upon me with a shower of mercy.

When grace is lost from life, come with a burst of song.

When tumultuous work raises its din on all sides shutting me out from beyond, come to me, my lord of silence, with thy peace and rest.

When my beggarly heart sits crouched, shut up in a corner, break open the door, my king, and come with the ceremony of a king.

When desire blinds the mind with delusion and dust, O thou holy one, thou wakeful, come with thy light and thy thunder.

39

当我的心冷酷干枯时，请为我降下慈悲的甘霖。

当生命失去恩宠时，请带给我激越的歌。

当无头序的琐事在四周喧闹，使我与上界隔绝时，我沉默的主，请带给我安宁与歇息。

当我赤贫的心蜷缩在一个角落时，我的国王，请你以王者的威仪破门而入吧。

当欲念用幻象与尘埃蒙蔽我的心时，啊，你这神圣者，你这警醒者，请你带来闪电与轰雷吧。

日复一日，没有雨降到我干旱的心。
天边赤裸得可怕。

The rain has held back for days and days, my God, in my arid heart. The horizon is fiercely naked—not the thinnest cover of a soft cloud, not the vaguest hint of a distant cool shower.

Send thy angry storm, dark with death, if it is thy wish, and with lashes of lightning startle the sky from end to end.

But call back, my lord, call back this pervading silent heat, still and keen and cruel, burning the heart with dire despair.

Let the cloud of grace bend low from above like the tearful look of the mother on the day of the father's wrath.

40

日复一日，没有雨降到我干旱的心，我的上主。天边赤裸得可怕——没有一丝柔云遮蔽，没有一丝凉雨遥远的影踪。

如果你愿意，请降下愤怒的暴雨，带着死亡的黑暗，以闪电之鞭震慑诸天吧。

但请召回，我的主，召回这四处弥漫、沉默的炎热吧，它死寂、锋利又残忍，用恐怖的绝望焚烧人心。

让慈云从天低垂而下，像父亲发怒那天，母亲含泪的目光。

我怎能告诉他们我在等候你，而且你答应我会来。

Where dost thou stand behind them all, my lover, hiding thyself in the shadows? They push thee and pass thee by on the dusty road, taking thee for naught. I wait here weary hours spreading my offerings for thee, while passers-by come and take my flowers, one by one, and my basket is nearly empty.

The morning time is past, and the noon. In the shade of evening my eyes are drowsy with sleep. Men going home glance at me and smile and fill me with shame. I sit like a beggar maid, drawing my skirt over my face, and when they ask me, what it is I want, I drop my eyes and answer them not.

Oh, how, indeed, could I tell them that for thee I wait, and that thou hast promised to come. How could I utter for shame that I keep for my dowry this poverty. Ah, I hug this pride in the secret of my heart.

41

藏在阴影中，你在众人身后站在何处，我的爱人？在尘土飞扬的道路上，他们推开你走过，不把你放在眼里。倦乏时分，我在此摆上供品等候你，过路行人一朵一朵地拿走我的花，我的花篮就要空了。

过了清晨，又过了正午。暮色中，我睡眼迷蒙。归家的人笑着瞥视我，使我满心羞愧。我像乞丐女般坐着，拉起裙子盖住脸，当他们问我要的是什么，我眼睛低垂不作答。

啊，真的，我怎能告诉他们我在等候你，而且你答应我会来。我怎能满脸羞愧地说，我用贫困做嫁妆。啊，我在心的隐秘处拥抱着这尊荣。

I sit on the grass and gaze upon the sky and dream of the sudden splendour of thy coming—all the lights ablaze, golden pennons flying over thy car, and they at the roadside standing agape, when they see thee come down from thy seat to raise me from the dust, and set at thy side this ragged beggar girl a-tremble with shame and pride, like a creeper in a summer breeze.

But time glides on and still no sound of the wheels of thy chariot. Many a procession passes by with noise and shouts and glamour of glory. Is it only thou who wouldst stand in the shadow silent and behind them all? And only I who would wait and weep and wear out my heart in vain longing?

我坐在草地上凝望天空，梦想着你突然来临的辉煌——万彩交辉，旌旗在你的车上飞扬，众人在路旁站着目瞪口呆。他们见你从车座上下驾，把我从尘土中扶起，让我坐在你身旁，这衣衫褴褛的乞丐女，又羞又喜，像蔓藤在夏日的和风中颤栗。

可是时间悄然逝去，还未传来你马车的轮声。许多列队都在辉煌耀眼的喧闹中走过。难道只有你静默地站在众人身后的阴影中？难道我只能哭泣着等待，在徒然的渴望中心力交瘁？

我们要去泛舟，只有你和我，世上绝无人知道我们这无目的、无终点的远游。

Early in the day it was whispered that we should sail in a boat, only thou and I, and never a soul in the world would know of this our pilgrimage to no country and to no end.

In that shoreless ocean, at thy silently listening smile my songs would swell in melodies, free as waves, free from all bondage of words.

Is the time not come yet? Are there works still to do? Lo, the evening has come down upon the shore and in the fading light the seabirds come flying to their nests.

Who knows when the chains will be off, and the boat, like the last glimmer of sunset, vanish into the night?

42

清早传来密语说，我们要去泛舟，只有你和我，世上绝无人知道我们这无目的、无终点的远游。

在那无边的大海上，在你静听的微笑中，我的歌曲激越，成为美妙旋律，像海浪般自由，不受任何字句的束缚。

那时刻还未到？还有活要干？看吧，暮色已笼罩海岸，光明正在消隐，海鸟正群飞归巢。

谁知道何时锁链会脱落，船儿会像落日的余晖消失在黑夜中？

你把永恒的印记，烙在我生命中许多飞逝的瞬间。

The day was when I did not keep myself in readiness for thee; and entering my heart unbidden even as one of the common crowd, unknown to me, my king, thou didst press the signet of eternity upon many a fleeting moment of my life.

And today when by chance I light upon them and see thy signature, I find they have lain scattered in the dust mixed with the memory of joys and sorrows of my trivial days forgotten.

Thou didst not turn in contempt from my childish play among dust, and the steps that I heard in my playroom are the same that are echoing from star to star.

43

那天我没有做好迎候你的准备，你不请自来进入我心中，就像素不相识芸芸众生的一员，我的王，你把永恒的印记，烙在我生命中许多飞逝的瞬间。

今天我偶然发现你的印记，我看到它们零乱地洒落在尘埃里，和被遗忘的琐碎日子的悲喜回忆混杂在一起。

你不曾鄙夷地转身不理睬我在尘土中幼稚的游戏，我在游戏室里听见的足音也同样回荡在群星中。

光影相逐，夏至雨来，就这样在路旁守望是我的快乐。

This is my delight, thus to wait and watch at the wayside where shadow chases light and the rain comes in the wake of the summer.

Messengers, with tidings from unknown skies, greet me and speed along the road. My heart is glad within, and the breath of the passing breeze is sweet.

From dawn till dusk I sit here before my door, and I know that of a sudden the happy moment will arrive when I shall see.

In the meanwhile I smile and I sing all alone. In the meanwhile the air is filling with the perfume of promise.

44

光影相逐，夏至雨来，就这样在路旁守望是我的快乐。

带着来自未知苍穹信息的使者们，招呼了我，又向前赶路。我内心欢畅，徐风吹过的气息带着香甜。

从清晨到黄昏，我在门前坐着，我知道一见到你，那快乐时光就会骤然而至。

此时，我独自高歌欢笑。此时，空气中充满了应许的芬芳。

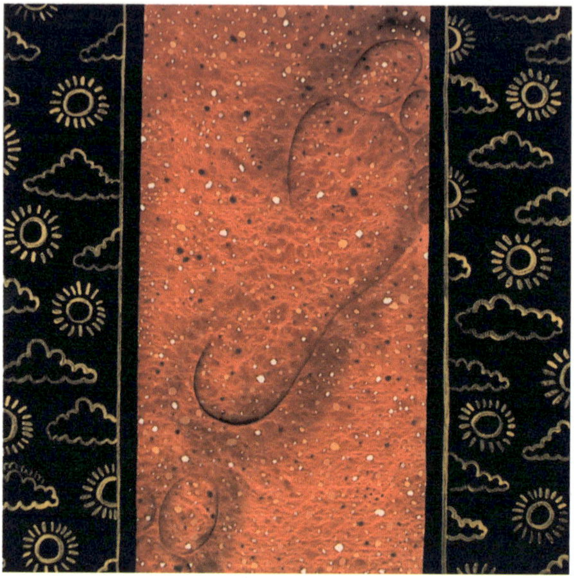

难道你还没听到他静悄悄的脚步？他正走来，走来，不停地走来。

Have you not heard his silent steps? He comes, comes, ever comes.

Every moment and every age, every day and every night he comes, comes, ever comes.

Many a song have I sung in many a mood of mind, but all their notes have always proclaimed, "He comes, comes, ever comes."

In the fragrant days of sunny April through the forest path he comes, comes, ever comes.

In the rainy gloom of July nights on the thundering chariot of clouds he comes, comes, ever comes.

In sorrow after sorrow it is his steps that press upon my heart, and it is the golden touch of his feet that makes my joy to shine.

45

难道你还没听到他静悄悄的脚步？他正走来，走来，不停地走来。

每个时刻，每个年代，每日每夜，他总在走来，走来，不停地走来。

在许多心绪下，我唱过许多歌，而它们所有的音符都在宣告：“他正走来，走来，不停地走来。”

明媚四月芬芳的日子，他从树林小径走来，走来，不停地走来。

七月夜雨的阴暗中，他坐着隆隆的云车奔来，奔来，不停地奔来。

在层出不穷的悲苦中，是他的脚步踏在我的心坎上，是他双脚金色的轻触，使我的喜悦放光芒。

你的太阳和星辰，不能永远把你藏起来，不让我看见你。

I know not from what distant time thou art ever coming nearer to meet me. Thy sun and stars can never keep thee hidden from me for aye.

In many a morning and eve thy footsteps have been heard and thy messenger has come within my heart and called me in secret.

I know not only why today my life is all astir, and a feeling of tremulous joy is passing through my heart.

It is as if the time were come to wind up my work, and I feel in the air a faint smell of thy sweet presence.

46

不知从什么久远的年代，你就一直走近我，来与我相会。你的太阳和星辰，不能永远把你藏起来，不让我看见你。

许多清晨和傍晚，我曾听见你的足音，你的使者曾来到我心中秘密召唤我。

不知为何单单今天我的生命充满了骚动，一阵颤栗的喜悦掠过我的心。

就像收工的时刻到了，我感觉空气中有一股你驾临时的馨香。

让他出现在我眼前，像所有最初的光和形。

The night is nearly spent waiting for him in vain. I fear lest in the morning he suddenly come to my door when I have fallen asleep wearied out. Oh friends, leave the way open to him—forbid him not.

If the sounds of his steps does not wake me, do not try to rouse me, I pray. I wish not to be called from my sleep by the clamorous choir of birds, by the riot of wind at the festival of morning light. Let me sleep undisturbed even if my lord comes of a sudden to my door.

Ah, my sleep, precious sleep, which only waits for his touch to vanish. Ah, my closed eyes that would open their lids only to the light of his smile when he stands before me like a dream emerging from darkness of sleep.

Let him appear before my sight as the first of all lights and all forms. The first thrill of joy to my awakened soul let it come from his glance. And let my return to myself be immediate return to him.

47

我几乎徒然地等了他一整夜。我担心万一清晨我正疲倦昏睡时，他突然驾临到我门前。啊，友人，让门开着——不要把他挡在门外。

要是他的脚步声没有使我醒来，请不要勉强把我叫醒。我不想被小鸟嘈杂的合唱和欢庆晨光喧闹的风声从睡梦中唤醒。让我睡着不受打扰，即使我的主突然驾临到我门前。

啊，我的睡眠，宝贵的睡眠，只等待他的触摸才消退。当他站在我面前，像一个梦从睡眠的黑暗中浮现，啊，我闭合的双眼，只在他微笑的光芒中才打开眼帘。

让他出现在我眼前，像所有最初的光和形。让他的一瞥带给我觉醒的灵魂第一次喜悦的颤栗。让我向自我的回归，即刻成为向他的皈依。

太阳升到中天，鸽子在阴凉处咕咕叫唤。枯叶在正午热气中盘旋飞舞。

The morning sea of silence broke into ripples of bird songs; and the flowers were all merry by the roadside; and the wealth of gold was scattered through the rift of the clouds while we busily went on our way and paid no heed.

We sang no glad songs nor played; we went not to the village for barter; we spoke not a word nor smiled; we lingered not on the way. We quickened our pace more and more as the time sped by.

The sun rose to the mid sky and doves cooed in the shade. Withered leaves danced and whirled in the hot air of noon. The shepherd boy drowsed and dreamed in the shadow of the banyan tree, and I laid myself down by the water and stretched my tired limbs on the grass.

48

清晨宁静的大海荡起鸟儿歌唱的涟漪；路边花儿都喜笑颜开；当我们匆忙赶路，不经意间，云层间洒下灿烂的金光。

我们没有欢声歌唱，也没有嬉戏；我们不到村里做交易；我们不作声，也不笑；我们不在路上留连。时间飞逝，我们的脚步也越来越快。

太阳升到中天，鸽子在阴凉处咕咕叫唤。枯叶在正午热气中盘旋飞舞。牧童在榕树的树荫下昏昏欲睡，进入梦乡，我在水边躺下，在草地上伸展我疲惫的四肢。

My companions laughed at me in scorn; they held their heads high and hurried on; they never looked back nor rested; they vanished in the distant blue haze. They crossed many meadows and hills, and passed through strange, far-away countries. All honour to you, heroic host of the interminable path!

Mockery and reproach pricked me to rise, but found no response in me. I gave myself up for lost in the depth of a glad humiliation—in the shadow of a dim delight.

The repose of the sun-embroidered green gloom slowly spread over my heart. I forgot for what I had travelled, and I surrendered my mind without struggle to the maze of shadows and songs.

At last, when I woke from my slumber and opened my eyes, I saw thee standing by me, flooding my sleep with thy smile. How I had feared that the path was long and wearisome, and the struggle to reach thee was hard!

同伴们嘲笑我；他们抬着头赶路；没有回望也没有休息；消失在远方蓝色薄雾中。他们穿过许多草地、山岗，走过陌生、遥远的疆域。征途上英勇的队伍啊，光荣全属于你们！

讥笑和责备催我起身，但我却没有反应。我放弃自己，迷失在乐于蒙羞的深处——在淡淡喜悦的阴影中。

阳光织成绿色昏暗的安眠，渐渐弥漫到我的心。我忘记了为何旅行，毫无挣扎地把我的神智交给阴影和歌曲的迷宫。

最后，我从沉睡中醒来，睁开眼睛，我看见你站在我的身旁，你的微笑淹没了我的睡眠。我曾多么害怕这道路漫长、令人疲倦，到你面前的奋斗有多艰难！

一曲忧郁的小调和世上伟大的音乐相融合，用一朵花儿作为奖赏，你走下来站在我小屋门前。

You came down from your throne and stood at my cottage door.

I was singing all alone in a corner, and the melody caught your ear. You came down and stood at my cottage door.

Masters are many in your hall, and songs are sung there at all hours. But the simple carol of this novice struck at your love. One plaintive little strain mingled with the great music of the world, and with a flower for a prize you came down and stopped at my cottage door.

49

你走下王座，站在我小屋门前。

我正在屋角独自歌唱，歌声传到你耳边。你走下来站在我小屋门前。

你的大厅里有许多出色的歌手，从早到晚歌声不绝。可这个新手单纯的颂唱触动了你。一曲忧郁的小调和世上伟大的音乐相融合，用一朵花儿作为奖赏，你走下来站在我小屋门前。

我痛哭了，真希望我心量大到把一切全都献给你。

I had gone a-begging from door to door in the village path, when thy golden chariot appeared in the distance like a gorgeous dream and I wondered who was this King of all kings!

My hopes rose high and methought my evil days were at an end, and I stood waiting for alms to be given unasked and for wealth scattered on all sides in the dust.

The chariot stopped where I stood. Thy glance fell on me and thou camest down with a smile. I felt that the luck of my life had come at last. Then of a sudden thou didst hold out thy right hand and say "What hast thou to give to me?"

50

在村子的小路上，我挨家挨户乞讨，你金色的马车出现在远处像一个华丽的梦，我心想这万王之王是谁呢！

我的希望升高，我想我不幸的日子将要结束，我站着等候施舍，不用问就给予，等着财宝散落在四周的尘土里。

马车停在我站立的地方。你的目光落到我身上，你微笑着走下车。我觉得我有生以来的好运终于到来了。忽然，你伸出右手说：“你有什么可以给我？”

Ah, what a kingly jest was it to open thy palm to a beggar to beg! I was confused and stood undecided, and then from my wallet I slowly took out the least little grain of corn and gave it to thee.

But how great my surprise when at the day's end I emptied my bag on the floor to find a least little gram of gold among the poor heap. I bitterly wept and wished that I had had the heart to give thee my all.

啊，开的是什么帝王的玩笑啊，竟向一个乞丐伸手求乞！我糊涂了，犹豫不决地站着，然后从口袋里，慢慢地掏出一颗最小的谷粒递给你。

当日终了，我把布袋倒空在地上，我大吃一惊，发现一粒金子在一堆破烂中。我痛哭了，真希望我心量大到把一切全都献给你。

雷声在天空咆哮，黑暗因闪电而颤抖。我们的国王在恐怖的夜里突然与风暴一同驾临了。

The night darkened. Our day's works had been done. We thought that the last guest had arrived for the night and the doors in the village were all shut. Only some said the king was to come. We laughed and said "No, it cannot be!"

It seemed there were knocks at the door and we said it was nothing but the wind. We put out the lamps and lay down to sleep. Only some said, "It is the messenger!" We laughed and said "No, it must be the wind!"

There came a sound in the dead of the night. We sleepily thought it was the distant thunder. The earth shook, the walls rocked, and it troubled us in our sleep. Only some said it was the sound of wheels. We said in a drowsy murmur, "No, it must be the rumbling of clouds!"

51

夜更深了。我们白天的活已经做完。我们以为投宿的旅人都已经到达，村里家家户户都关上了门。可是有人说国王要来。我们大笑说：“不，这不可能！”

好像有人在敲门，我们说那只是风。我们熄了灯躺下睡觉。只是有人说：“使者来了！”我们大笑说：“不可能，那一定是风！”

沉寂的深夜里传来一个声音。睡眼蒙眬中，我们以为那是遥远的雷鸣。地震墙摇，我们在睡梦中受到惊扰。可是有人说那是车轮的声音。我们在昏睡中嘟哝着说：“不，那一定是云层的喧嚷！”

The night was still dark when the drum sounded. The voice came "Wake up! delay not!" We pressed our hands on our hearts and shuddered with fear. Some said, "Lo, there is the king's flag!" We stood up on our feet and cried "There is no time for delay!"

The king has come—but where are lights, where are wreaths? Where is the throne to seat him? Oh, shame! Oh utter shame! Where is the hall, the decorations? Someone has said, "Vain is this cry! Greet him with empty hands, lead him into thy rooms all bare!"

Open the doors, let the conch-shells be sounded! In the depth of the night has come the king of our dark, dreary house. The thunder roars in the sky. The darkness shudders with lightning. Bring out thy tattered piece of mat and spread it in the courtyard. With the storm has come of a sudden our king of the fearful night.

鼓声响起，夜还是一片黑暗。有一个声音传来：“醒来！别磨蹭了！”我们用手按住心口，吓得发抖。有人说：“看哪，那是国王的旗帜！”我们站起来，喊道：“没有时间磨蹭了！”

国王已经到来了——可是灯在哪里，花环在哪里？给他坐的宝座在哪里？啊，丢脸！啊，真丢脸！客厅在哪里，摆设在哪里？有一个人说：“叫有何用！空手来迎接他，把他带到你空荡荡的屋子里吧！”

打开门，吹起海螺吧！深夜里国王驾临到我们黑暗凄凉的屋子。雷声在天空咆哮。黑暗因闪电而颤抖。拿出你破旧的垫子铺在院子里吧。我们的国王在恐怖的夜里突然与风暴一同驾临了。

我要用你的宝剑斩断我的镣铐，在这世上我将无所畏惧。

I thought I should ask of thee—but I dared not—the rose wreath thou hadst on thy neck. Thus I waited for the morning, when thou didst depart, to find a few fragments on the bed. And like a beggar I searched in the dawn only for a stray petal or two.

Ah me, what is it I find? What token left of thy love? It is no flower, no spices, no vase of perfumed water. It is thy mighty sword, flashing as a flame, heavy as a bolt of thunder. The young light of morning comes through the window and spread itself upon thy bed. The morning bird twitters and asks, "Woman, what hast thou got?" No, it is no flower, nor spices, nor vase of perfumed water—it is thy dreadful sword.

52

我想向你要——可是我不敢——你挂在颈上的玫瑰花环。因此，我等到早晨，当你离开后，从你床上找一些碎片。像一个乞丐，黎明时分我就来寻找，只为了一两片散落的花瓣。

啊，我啊，我要找的是什么呢？你的爱人留下什么信物？不是花，不是香料，也不是一瓶香水。而是你的巨大宝剑，火焰般闪耀，雷霆般沉重。晨曦透过窗户洒到你的床上。晨鸟啁啾地问道：“女人，你找到了什么？”不，不是花朵，不是香料，也不是一瓶香水——而是你可怕的宝剑。

I sit and muse in wonder, what gift is this of thine. I can find no place to hide it. I am ashamed to wear it, frail as I am, and it hurts me when press it to my bosom. Yet shall I bear in my heart this honour of the burden of pain, this gift of thine.

From now there shall be no fear left for me in this world, and thou shalt be victorious in all my strife. Thou hast left death for my companion and I shall crown him with my life. Thy sword is with me to cut asunder my bonds, and there shall be no fear left for me in the world.

From now I leave off all petty decorations. Lord of my heart, no more shall there be for me waiting and weeping in corners, no more coyness and sweetness of demeanour. Thou hast given me thy sword for adornment. No more doll's decorations for me!

我在惊异中静坐沉思，你这礼物是什么。我找不到藏放它的地方。我不好意思佩带它；我这么柔弱，我把它抱紧在胸前，它会伤到我。可我要在心中背起你的礼物，这痛苦重负的荣耀。

今后，在这世上我将无所畏惧，在我的一切奋斗中你必得胜。你留下死亡与我做伴，我将用生命冠冕他。我要用你的宝剑斩断我的镣铐，在这世上我将无所畏惧。

今后，我要抛弃一切琐碎的装饰。我心灵的主，我再也不会在角落等待、哭泣，再也不会羞怯、举止温柔。你已把你的宝剑给我做装饰。我再也不需要玩偶做饰品了！

它闪耀着，像生命纯洁的火焰，用猛烈的一闪燃尽尘世的情感。

Beautiful is thy wristlet, decked with stars and cunningly wrought in myriad-coloured jewels. But more beautiful to me thy sword with its curve of lightning like the outspread wings of the divine bird of Vishnu, perfectly poised in the angry red light of the sunset.

It quivers like the one last response of life in ecstasy of pain at the final stroke of death; it shines like the pure flame of being burning up earthly sense with one fierce flash.

Beautiful is thy wristlet, decked with starry gems; but thy sword, O lord of thunder, is wrought with uttermost beauty, terrible to behold or think of.

53

你的手镯真美丽，镶嵌着星辰，精巧地装饰着各色珠宝。但我觉得你的宝剑更美丽，它那弧形的闪光像毗湿奴的神鸟伸展着翅膀，完美地平衡在落日怒发的红光里。

它颤抖着，像生命受死亡最后一击，在痛苦狂迷中的临终反应；它闪耀着，像生命纯洁的火焰，用猛烈的一闪燃尽尘世的情感。

你的手镯真美丽，镶嵌着星辰般的珠宝；而你的宝剑，啊，雷霆之主，锻造得绝顶美丽，看到、想到都令人畏惧。

树叶在头顶上沙沙作响，杜鹃躲在人们看不见的幽暗处歌唱，胶树花香从曲径飘来。

I asked nothing from thee; I uttered not my name to thine ear. When thou took'st thy leave I stood silent. I was alone by the well where the shadow of the tree fell aslant, and the women had gone home with their brown earthen pitchers full to the brim. They called me and shouted, "Come with us, the morning is wearing on to noon." But I languidly lingered awhile lost in the midst of vague musings.

I heard not thy steps as thou camest. Thine eyes were sad when they fell on me; thy voice was tired as thou spokest low—"Ah, I am a thirsty traveller." I started up from my day-dreams and poured water from my jar on thy joined palms. The leaves rustled overhead; the cuckoo sang from the unseen dark, and perfume of *babla* flowers came from the bend of the road.

54

我不向你要什么；我不向你耳边唠叨我的名字。当你离去时，我静静地站着。我独自在树影斜荫的水井旁，女人们已顶着盛满水的褐色瓦罐回家了。她们向我高声说：“和我们一起走吧，中午快到了。”可我慵倦地留连片刻，沉入茫然的冥想中。

我没有听到你来时的足音。你看我时眼里带着伤感；你低声说话时声音显得疲倦——“啊，我是个干渴的旅人。”我从白日睡梦中惊醒，把水从水罐里倒在你合拢的手掌上。树叶在头顶上沙沙作响，杜鹃躲在人们看不见的幽暗处歌唱，胶树花香从曲径飘来。

I stood speechless with shame when my name thou didst ask. Indeed, what had I done for thee to keep me in remembrance? But the memory that I could give water to thee to allay thy thirst will cling to my heart and enfold it in sweetness. The morning hour is late, the bird sings in weary notes, *neem* leaves rustle overhead and I sit and think and think.

当你问起我的名字时，我站着羞愧得说不出话。真的，我为你做了什么使你记得我？但我给你饮水止渴的记忆，将紧贴在我的心，甜蜜地抱紧它。早晨就要过去，鸟儿疲倦地歌唱，头顶上楝树的叶子沙沙作响，我坐着联翩浮想。

难道你没有听说荆棘丛中花儿称霸，辉煌耀眼吗？醒来吧，啊，醒来！不要让光阴虚度！

Languor is upon your heart and the slumber is still on your eyes.

Has not the word come to you that the flower is reigning in splendour among thorns? Wake, oh awaken! Let not the time pass in vain!

At the end of the stony path, in the country of virgin solitude, my friend is sitting all alone. Deceive him not. Wake, oh awaken!

What if the sky pants and trembles with the heat of the midday sun—what if the burning sand spreads its mantle of thirst—

Is there no joy in the deep of your heart? At every footfall of yours, will not the harp of the road break out in sweet music of pain?

55

你的心充满倦息，你的眼睛还带着睡意。

难道你没有听说荆棘丛中花儿称霸，辉煌耀眼吗？醒来吧，啊，醒来！不要让光阴虚度！

在石径的尽头，在僻静无人的乡野，我的朋友独自坐着。不要欺骗他。醒来，啊，醒来吧！

即使正午的骄阳使天空喘息、颤抖——即使灼热的黄沙展开它干渴的斗篷——

你的心灵深处难道没有喜悦吗？你的每一个足音，难道不会使道路的竖琴迸发出痛楚而美妙的音乐吗？

你的爱迷失在你爱人的爱里，在那里，
你以两者完美的结合显现。

Thus it is that thy joy in me is so full. Thus it is that thou hast come down to me. O thou lord of all heavens, where would be thy love if I were not?

Thou hast taken me as thy partner of all this wealth. In my heart is the endless play of thy delight. In my life thy will is ever taking shape.

And for this, thou who art the King of kings hast decked thyself in beauty to captivate my heart. And for this thy love loses itself in the love of thy lover, and there art thou seen in the perfect union of two.

56

就这样，你的喜悦如此充满我的内心。就这样，你曾经驾临到我身边。啊，你这诸天之主，假如不是我，你会爱谁呢?

你已把我当作你一切财富的分享者。你的欢乐在我心里不停嬉闹。你的意愿在我生命中不断形成。

为此，你这万王之王曾经打扮自己来赢得我的心。为此，你的爱迷失在你爱人的爱里，在那里，你以两者完美的结合显现。

光明在每朵云上散成黄金，亲爱的，
它洒下无数珍宝。

Light, my light, the world-filling light, the eye-kissing light, heart-sweetening light!

Ah, the light dances, my darling, at the centre of my life; the light strikes, my darling, the chords of my love; the sky opens, the wind runs wild, laughter passes over the earth.

The butterflies spread their sails on the sea of light. Lilies and jasmines surge up on the crest of the waves of light.

The light is shattered into gold on every cloud, my darling, and it scatters gems in profusion.

Mirth spreads from leaf to leaf, my darling, and gladness without measure. The heaven's river has drowned its banks and the flood of joy is abroad.

57

光明，我的光明，充满世界的光明，亲吻眼睛的光明，沁人心脾的光明！

啊，亲爱的，光明在我生命的中心舞蹈；亲爱的，光明在弹拨我爱的心弦；天门打开了，狂风大作，欢声传遍大地。

蝴蝶在光明之海展翅扬帆。百合与茉莉在光明的浪尖翻涌。

光明在每朵云上散成黄金，亲爱的，它洒下无数珍宝。

亲爱的，欢笑在树叶间蔓延，喜悦无边。天河的堤岸被淹没了，欢乐的洪水四处奔流。

那欢乐含泪静坐在盛开的痛苦红莲上，那欢乐把它拥有的一切扔在尘土中，毫不自知。

Let all the strains of joy mingle in my last song—the joy that makes the earth flow over in the riotous excess of the grass, the joy that sets the twin brothers, life and death, dancing over the wide world, the joy that sweeps in with the tempest, shaking and waking all life with laughter, the joy that sits still with its tears on the open red lotus of pain, and the joy that throws everything it has upon the dust, and knows not a word.

58

让所有欢乐的曲调都融入我最后的歌——那欢乐使草儿狂欢，大地涌动，那欢乐使生死这对孪生兄弟在广阔的世界舞蹈，那欢乐和风暴一同卷来，笑声震撼、惊醒一切生命，那欢乐含泪静坐在盛开的痛苦红莲上，那欢乐把它拥有的一切扔在尘土中，毫不自知。

这一定是你的爱，啊，我心爱的人——这树叶上舞蹈的金色阳光，这掠过天空的悠闲云朵。

Yes, I know, this is nothing but thy love, O beloved of my heart—this golden light that dances upon the leaves, these idle clouds sailing across the sky, this passing breeze leaving its coolness upon my forehead.

The morning light has flooded my eyes—this is thy message to my heart. Thy face is bent from above, thy eyes look down on my eyes, and my heart has touched thy feet.

59

是的，我明白，这一定是你的爱，啊，我心爱的人——这树叶上舞蹈的金色阳光，这掠过天空的悠闲云朵，这使我额头凉爽的徐风。

晨光注满了我的眼睛——这是你给我的心捎来的信息。你俯下脸孔，眼睛往下望着我的眼睛，我的心触到了你的双脚。

头上是沉静无垠的天空，不平静的海水汹涌澎湃。无穷世界的岸边，孩子们相聚，欢声雀跃。

On the seashore of endless worlds children meet. The infinite sky is motionless overhead and the restless water is boisterous. On the seashore of endless worlds the children meet with shouts and dances.

They build their houses with sand and they play with empty shells. With withered leaves they weave their boats and smilingly float them on the vast deep. Children have their play on the seashore of worlds.

They know not how to swim, they know not how to cast nets. Pearl fishers dive for pearls, merchants sail in their ships, while children gather pebbles and scatter them again. They seek not for hidden treasures, they know not how to cast nets.

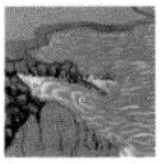

60

无穷世界的岸边，孩子们相聚。头上是沉静无垠的天空，不平静的海水汹涌澎湃。无穷世界的岸边，孩子们相聚，欢声雀跃。

他们用沙子盖起房子，用贝壳来玩耍。他们把枯叶编成小船，微笑着把它们漂浮在深广的海上。无穷世界的岸边，孩子们玩耍着。

他们不知道怎么游泳，也不知道怎么撒网。采珠人潜水采珠，商人们乘船航行，可孩子们把卵石聚起又将它们打散。他们不寻找隐藏的珍宝，不知道怎么撒网。

The sea surges up with laughter and pale gleams the smile of the sea beach. Death-dealing waves sing meaningless ballads to the children, even like a mother while rocking her baby's cradle. The sea plays with children, and pale gleams the smile of the sea beach.

On the seashore of endless worlds children meet. Tempest roams in the pathless sky, ships get wrecked in the trackless water, death is abroad and children play. On the seashore of endless worlds is the great meeting of children.

大海涌起了笑声，海滩闪烁着苍白的微笑。致人死命的浪涛对孩子们唱着毫无意义的歌谣，甚至像母亲摇着婴儿的摇篮。大海和孩子们玩耍，海滩闪烁着苍白的微笑。

无穷世界的岸边，孩子们相聚。风暴在无路的天空漫游，船舶在无轨的海上沉没，死亡遍布，孩子们却在玩耍。无穷世界的岸边，孩子们在大聚会。

相传，一线新月初生的柔光，接触到正在消逝的秋云边缘，那里，微笑首次诞生在露水洗过的清晨梦中。

The sleep that flits on baby's eyes—does anybody know from where it comes? Yes, there is a rumour that it has its dwelling where, in the fairy village among shadows of the forest dimly lit with glow-worms, there hang two timid buds of enchantment. From there it comes to kiss baby's eyes.

The smile that flickers on baby's lips when he sleeps—does anybody know where it was born? Yes, there is a rumour that a young pale beam of a crescent moon touched the edge of a vanishing autumn cloud, and there the smile was first born in the dream of a dew-washed morning—the smile that flickers on baby's lips when he sleeps.

The sweet, soft freshness that blooms on baby's limbs—does anybody know where it was hidden so long? Yes, when the mother was a young girl it lay pervading her heart in tender and silent mystery of love—the sweet, soft freshness that has bloomed on baby's limbs.

61

那掠过婴儿眼睛的睡眠——有谁知道它来自哪里？有，相传它住在森林阴影中的仙村里，萤火虫微光闪烁，那里挂着两颗迷幻羞怯的花蕾。从那里，它来亲吻婴儿的眼睛。

那睡梦中婴儿唇上闪现的微笑——有谁知道它生自哪里？有，相传，一线新月初生的柔光，接触到正在消逝的秋云边缘，那里，微笑首次诞生在露水洗过的清晨梦中——那睡梦中婴儿唇上闪现的微笑。

那从婴儿四肢上散发出的甜蜜温柔的清新——有谁知道它在哪里藏了这么久？有，当母亲还是一个少女时，它就在温柔、宁静的爱之神秘中，占据并充满了她的心——那从婴儿四肢散发出来的甜蜜温柔的清新。

当我把糖果递到你贪心的手中时，我才懂得为何花心有蜜，为何水果秘密地充满甜汁。

When I bring to you coloured toys, my child, I understand why there is such a play of colours on clouds, on water, and why flowers are painted in tints—when I give coloured toys to you, my child.

When I sing to make you dance I truly know why there is music in leaves, and why waves send their chorus of voices to the heart of the listening earth—when I sing to make you dance.

When I bring sweet things to your greedy hands I know why there is honey in the cup of the flowers and why fruits are secretly filled with sweet juice—when I bring sweet things to your greedy hands.

When I kiss your face to make you smile, my darling, I surely understand what pleasure streams from the sky in morning light, and what delight that is which the summer breeze brings to my body—when I kiss you to make you smile.

62

当我送你多彩的玩具时，我的孩子，我才理解为何云中、水上有如此变幻莫测的色彩，为何花朵都染上颜色——当我送你多彩的玩具时，我的孩子。

当我歌唱使你跳起舞时，我才真正知道为何树叶发出音乐，为何波浪把合唱传送给大地倾听的心——当我歌唱使你跳起舞时。

当我把糖果递到你贪心的手中时，我才懂得为何花心有蜜，为何水果秘密地充满甜汁——当我把糖果递到你贪心的手中时。

当我亲吻你的脸使你微笑时，我亲爱的，我才完全理解晨光从天空倾泻而下是什么快乐，夏日和风吹到我身上是什么快乐——当我亲吻你的脸使你微笑时。

一旦认识你，就不再有陌生的人，就不会有紧闭的门。

Thou hast made me known to friends whom I knew not. Thou hast given me seats in homes not my own. Thou hast brought the distant near and made a brother of the stranger.

I am uneasy at heart when I have to leave my accustomed shelter; I forget that there abides the old in the new, and that there also thou abidest.

Through birth and death, in this world or in others, wherever thou leadest me it is thou, the same, the one companion of my endless life who ever linkest my heart with bonds of joy to the unfamiliar.

When one knows thee, then alien there is none, then no door is shut. Oh, grant me my prayer that I may never lose the bliss of the touch of the one in the play of many.

63

你使我和素不相识的人成为朋友。你在别人家里给我留有座位。你使距离缩短，使陌生人成为兄弟。

当我不得不离开我习以为常的居所时，我心里不安；我没想到，在那里旧人住进新居，而且你也住在那里。

通过生和死，今生还是来世，无论你带我到哪里，总是你，同样的你，我无穷生命中唯一的伴侣，永远用喜悦的锁链把我的心和陌生的事物相连。

一旦认识你，就不再有陌生的人，就不会有紧闭的门。啊，请答应我的祈祷，在与众人的玩耍中，让我永远不会失去与你亲近的福祉。

她说，『要在白昼在西边消隐时，把我的灯漂在河上。』

On the slope of the desolate river among tall grasses I asked her, "Maiden, where do you go shading your lamp with your mantle? My house is all dark and lonesome—lend me your light!" she raised her dark eyes for a moment and looked at my face through the dusk. "I have come to the river," she said, "to float my lamp on the stream when the daylight wanes in the west." I stood alone among tall grasses and watched the timid flame of her lamp uselessly drifting in the tide.

In the silence of gathering night I asked her, "Maiden, your lights are all lit—then where do you go with your lamp? My house is all dark and lonesome—lend me your light." She raised her dark eyes on my face and stood for a moment doubtful. "I have come," she said at last, "to dedicate my lamp to the sky." I stood and watched her light uselessly burning in the void.

64

在荒凉河流的斜岸上，深草丛中，我问她：“姑娘，你用披风遮着灯，要往何处去？我的房子多么黑暗、寂寞——把你的灯借给我吧！”她抬起乌黑的眼睛，在暮色中朝我看了片刻。“我到河边来，”她说，“要在白昼在西边消隐时，把我的灯漂到河上。”我独自站在深草丛中，眼看着她微弱的灯光，徒然漂流在水波上。

在暮色渐深的寂静中，我问她：“你的灯都点上了——那么你要拿着灯往何处去？我的房子多么黑暗、寂寞——把你的灯借给我吧。”她抬起乌黑的眼睛望着我的脸，站着迟疑了片刻。最后她说：“我是来把我的灯献给天空的。”我站着，眼看着她的灯，徒然燃烧在虚空中。

In the moonless gloom of midnight I ask her, "Maiden, what is your quest, holding the lamp near your heart? My house is all dark and lonesome—lend me your light." She stopped for a minute and thought and gazed at my face in the dark. "I have brought my light," she said, "to join the carnival of lamps." I stood and watched her little lamp uselessly lost among lights.

在无月夜半的朦胧中，我问她：“姑娘，把灯举在胸前，你要找什么呢？我的房子多么黑暗、寂寞——把你的灯借给我吧。”她停步沉思了片刻，在黑暗中注视着我的脸。她说：“我带着我的灯来参加灯节。”我站着，眼看她小小的灯，徒然消失在灯海中。

你在爱中把自己给了我，又在我身上
感觉你自己全部的甜蜜。

What divine drink wouldst thou have, my God, from this overflowing cup of my life?

My poet, is it thy delight to see thy creation through my eyes and to stand at the portals of my ears silently to listen to thine own eternal harmony?

Thy world is weaving words in my mind and thy joy is adding music to them. Thou givest thyself to me in love and then feelest thine own entire sweetness in me.

65

我的上主，从我四溢的生命之杯，你要饮什么神圣的酒呢?

通过我的眼睛看你的造物，静静地站在我的耳门边，倾听你自己永恒的谐音，我的诗人，这是你的快乐吗?

你的世界在我的心里编织词句，你的喜悦给它们谱上曲子。你在爱中把自己给了我，又在我身上感觉你自己全部的甜蜜。

把她藏在深心里，我浪迹天涯，我生命的枯荣围绕着她起落。

She who ever had remained in the depth of my being, in the twilight of gleams and of glimpses; she who never opened her veils in the morning light, will be my last gift to thee, my God, folded in my final song.

Words have wooed yet failed to win her; persuasion has stretched to her its eager arms in vain.

I have roamed from country to country keeping her in the core of my heart, and around her have risen and fallen the growth and decay of my life.

Over my thoughts and actions, my slumbers and dreams, she reigned yet dwelled alone and apart.

Many a man knocked at my door and asked for her and turned away in despair.

There was none in the world who ever saw her face to face, and she remained in her loneliness waiting for thy recognition.

66

在微光隐约的黄昏，那一直留在我生命深处的她，那在晨光中永远不肯揭开面纱的她，我将用最后一首歌把她包裹起来，作为我给你的最后献礼，我的上主。

求爱的话语绵绵，却没有赢得她的心；劝诱徒然向她伸出渴望的臂膀。

把她藏在深心里，我浪迹天涯，我生命的枯荣围绕着她起落。

她统治着我的思想、行动、睡眠和梦境，自己却离群索居。

许多人来敲我的门寻找她，都失望地回去。

这世上从来没有人面对面见过她，她待在孤寂中等待你的赏识。

你的爱就在鸟巢里，它用色彩、声音和芳香围护着灵魂。

Thou art the sky and thou art the nest as well.

O thou beautiful, there in the nest is thy love that encloses the soul with colours and sounds and odours.

There comes the morning with the golden basket in her right hand bearing the wreath of beauty, silently to crown the earth.

And there comes the evening over the lonely meadows deserted by herds, through trackless paths, carrying cool draughts of peace in her golden pitcher from the western ocean of rest.

But there, where spreads the infinite sky for the soul to take her flight in, reigns the stainless white radiance. There is no day nor night, nor form nor colour, and never, never a word.

67

你是天空，你也是鸟巢。

啊，美丽的你，你的爱就在鸟巢里，它用色彩、声音和芳香围护着灵魂。

清晨从那里走来，右手提着金色的篮子，带着美丽花环，静静地为大地加冕。

黄昏从那里走来，越过无人放牧的荒凉草原，穿过人迹罕至的小径，携着她的金色酒罐，装着寂静西方之海的和平佳酿。

可是在那里，无瑕洁白的光辉统治着，无垠的天空为灵魂的翱翔展开着。那里，无昼无夜，无形无色，永远，永远一言不语。

带着温情的欣喜，你将这朦胧云彩的斗篷裹在你星光灿烂的胸脯上。

Thy sunbeam comes upon this earth of mine with arms outstretched and stands at my door the livelong day to carry back to thy feet clouds made of my tears and sighs and songs.

With fond delight thou wrappest about thy starry breast that mantle of misty cloud, turning it into numberless shapes and folds and colouring it with hues everchanging.

It is so light and so fleeting, tender and tearful and dark, that is why thou lovest it, O thou spotless and serene. And that is why it may cover thy awful white light with its pathetic shadows.

68

你的光线照在我的土地上，整天伸着臂膀站在我门前，把我的眼泪、叹息和歌声化成的云彩带回你的脚边。

带着温情的欣喜，你将这朦胧云彩的斗篷裹在你星光灿烂的胸脯上，把它绕成无数形状和皱褶，并染上变化无穷的色彩。

它是如此轻盈，如此飘扬、温柔、含泪且暗淡，这就是你爱它的原由，啊，你这庄严和无瑕者。这就是它能以令人怜悯的阴影遮盖你可怕光芒的原由。

同一股生命的川流日夜流经我的血管，也流经这世界，随着节律跳起舞。

The same stream of life that runs through my veins night and day runs through the world and dances in rhythmic measures.

It is the same life that shoots in joy through the dust of the earth in numberless blades of grass and breaks into tumultuous waves of leaves and flowers.

It is the same life that is rocked in the ocean-cradle of birth and of death, in ebb and in flow.

I feel my limbs are made glorious by the touch of this world of life. And my pride is from the life-throb of ages dancing in my blood this moment.

69

同一股生命的川流日夜流经我的血管，也流经这世界，随着节律跳起舞。

同样的生命从大地尘土里，喜悦地萌生出无数片芳草，迸发出花与叶的欢腾浪花。

同样的生命在潮涨潮落中，被摇荡在生和死的大海摇篮里。

我觉得我的四肢受到这生命世界的爱抚而显得荣耀。我的骄傲来自时代的生命脉搏，此刻正搏动在我的血液里。

颜色、旋律和芳香，在这丰裕的喜悦里倾注成无尽的瀑布，时刻飞溅、退落和消失。

Is it beyond thee to be glad with the gladness of this rhythm? to be tossed and lost and broken in the whirl of this fearful joy?

All things rush on, they stop not, they look not behind, no power can hold them back, they rush on.

Keeping steps with that restless, rapid music, seasons come dancing and pass away—colours, tunes, and perfumes pour in endless cascades in the abounding joy that scatters and gives up and dies every moment.

70

这韵律的欢快会使你禁不住地欣喜吗？你会禁不住地被摇荡、消失和打碎在这可怕喜悦的漩涡里吗？

万物向前奔腾，不停留，也不回顾，任何力量都不能阻止它们，它们向前奔腾。

和着这迅急不安的音乐，季节的脚步舞蹈而来又离去——颜色、旋律和芳香，在这丰裕的喜悦里倾注成无尽的瀑布，时刻飞溅、退落和消失。

你在自己的生命中设置阻隔，用无数特征来称呼你隔离的自我。

That I should make much of myself and turn it on all sides, thus casting coloured shadows on thy radiance—such is thy *maya*.

Thou settest a barrier in thine own being and then callest thy severed self in myriad notes. This thy self-separation has taken body in me.

The poignant song is echoed through all the sky in many-coloured tears and smiles, alarms and hopes; waves rise up and sink again, dreams break and form. In me is thy own defeat of self.

This screen that thou hast raised is painted with innumerable figures with the brush of the night and the day. Behind it thy seat is woven in wondrous mysteries of curves, casting away all barren lines of straightness.

The great pageant of thee and me has overspread the sky. With the tune of thee and me all the air is vibrant, and all ages pass with the hiding and seeking of thee and me.

71

我要极力宣扬自己、远播四方，在你的光芒中投下斑斓的阴影——这便是你的幻境。

你在自己的生命中设置阻隔，用无数特征来称呼你隔离的自我。你这隔离的自我形成了我的躯体。

刺耳的歌声以多彩的眼泪与微笑、震惊与希望在空中四处回荡；潮起潮落，梦想破灭又形成。在我身上你自己击败了自我。

你拉起的帘子上有白昼与黑夜的画笔画出的无数图案。帘子后面，你的座位用奇妙神秘的曲线织成，抛弃一切单调笔直的线条。

你我的盛典蔓延到天空。你我的曲调使四周空气震颤，在你我的捉迷藏中，一切时代逝去了。

正是他，用金、银、青、绿转瞬即逝的色彩织起幻境的网。

He it is, the innermost one, who awakens my being with his deep hidden touches.

He it is who puts his enchantment upon these eyes and joyfully plays on the chords of my heart in varied cadence of pleasure and pain.

He it is who weaves the web of this *maya* in evanescent hues of gold and silver, blue and green, and lets peep out through the folds his feet, at whose touch I forget myself.

Days come and ages pass, and it is ever he who moves my heart in many a name, in many a guise, in many a rapture of joy and of sorrow.

72

正是他，最深处的他，用他深藏的爱抚唤醒了我的生命。

正是他，把符咒放在我的眼睛上，又快乐地在我的心弦上弹出各种喜悦和悲痛的曲调。

正是他，用金、银、青、绿转瞬即逝的色彩织起幻境的网，他把脚露出衣褶外，在他的轻触下，我忘却了我自己。

时日匆匆，时代变换，永远是他以种种名字，种种伪装，种种狂喜和悲伤，来打动我的心。

我的世界将用你的火焰点上千百盏不同的灯，放在你殿宇的祭坛前。

Deliverance is not for me in renunciation. I feel the embrace of freedom in a thousand bonds of delight.

Thou ever pourest for me the fresh draught of thy wine of various colours and fragrance, filling this earthen vessel to the brim.

My world will light its hundred different lamps with thy flame and place them before the altar of thy temple.

No, I will never shut the doors of my senses. The delights of sight and hearing and touch will bear thy delight.

Yes, all my illusions will burn into illumination of joy, and all my desires ripen into fruits of love.

73

我不想了断尘缘寻求解脱。在无数快乐的束缚里我感到自由的拥抱。

你不断为我倒出你有各种香味和颜色的新酒，充满我的陶杯。

我的世界将用你的火焰点上千百盏不同的灯，放在你殿宇的祭坛前。

不，我永不会关上我的感觉之门。视觉、听觉、触觉的快乐会携带你的快乐。

是的，我一切幻想会燃烧成快乐的光明，我一切欲望会结成爱的果实。

荒凉的小径上没有行人，起风了，河面泛起涟漪。

The day is no more, the shadow is upon the earth. It is time that I go to the stream to fill my pitcher.

The evening air is eager with the sad music of the water. Ah, it calls me out into the dusk. In the lonely lane there is no passer-by, the wind is up, the ripples are rampant in the river.

I know not if I shall come back home. I know not whom I shall chance to meet. There at the fording in the little boat the unknown man plays upon his lute.

74

白昼已尽，阴影笼罩大地。我该到河边用瓦罐汲水了。

晚风随着水流忧伤的音乐流露着渴望。啊，它呼唤我出门走进暮色中。荒凉的小径上没有行人，起风了，河面泛起涟漪。

我不知道是否该回家。我不知道会邂逅谁。渡口小舟上有个不相识的人在弹琵琶。

花朵用芬芳使空气香甜；可它最后的礼拜仪式是把自己献给你。

Thy gifts to us mortals fulfil all our needs and yet run back to thee undiminished.

The river has its everyday work to do and hastens through fields and hamlets; yet its incessant stream winds towards the washing of thy feet.

The flower sweetens the air with its perfume; yet its last service is to offer itself to thee.

Thy worship does not impoverish the world.

From the words of the poet men take what meanings please them; yet their last meaning points to thee.

75

你赐予我们世人的礼物满足了我们所有需求，又丝毫不减地返回你那里。

小河有它日常要做的事，匆忙穿过田野和村庄；它不绝的流水又蜿蜒流向你，冲洗你的双脚。

花朵用芬芳使空气香甜；可它最后的礼拜仪式是把自己献给你。

对你的膜拜不会使世界变穷困。

人们从诗人的字里行间随心取意；但诗句的终极意义指向你。

在广阔孤寂的天空下，我能否带着谦卑的心与你相对站立？

Day after day, O lord of my life, shall I stand before thee face to face? With folded hands, O lord of all worlds, shall I stand before thee face to face?

Under thy great sky in solitude and silence, with humble heart shall I stand before thee face to face?

In this laborious world of thine, tumultuous with toil and with struggle, among hurrying crowds shall I stand before thee face to face?

And when my work shall be done in this world, O King of kings, alone and speechless shall I stand before thee face to face?

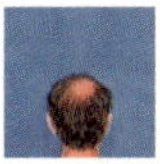

76

一天又一天，啊，我生命的主，我能否与你相对站立？啊，大千世界的主，我能否合掌与你相对站立？

在广阔孤寂的天空下，我能否带着谦卑的心与你相对站立？

在你这劳碌的世界里，喧嚣着辛劳与挣扎，我能否在匆忙的人群中与你相对站立？

当我今世的劳作终了时，啊，万王之王，我能否独自无言与你相对站立？

我畏缩着不想舍弃生命，因此我没有跳进生命的大潮里。

I know thee as my God and stand apart—I do not know thee as my own and come closer. I know thee as my father and bow before thy feet—I do not grasp thy hand as my friend's.

I stand not where thou comest down and ownest thyself as mine, there to clasp thee to my heart and take thee as my comrade.

Thou art the Brother amongst my brothers, but I heed them not, I divide not my earnings with them, thus sharing my all with thee.

In pleasure and in pain I stand not by the side of men, and thus stand by thee. I shrink to give up my life, and thus do not plunge into the great waters of life.

77

我知道你是我的主，就站得远远的——我不知道你是我自己的，就走近你。我知道你是我的父亲，就跪拜在你脚前——我没有紧握你的手把你当成朋友。

我没有站在你降临的地方，把你当成我的，没有在那里紧紧拥抱你，把你当成我的同伴。

你是我兄弟中最独特的一位，可我不理睬他们，不把我的所得分享给他们，这样我就能把一切与你分享。

无论快乐与苦痛，我都没有站在人这一边，这样才能和你站在一起。我畏缩着不想舍弃生命，因此我没有跳进生命的大潮里。

混沌初开，繁星初现，灿烂光辉。

When the creation was new and all the stars shone in their first splendour, the gods held their assembly in the sky and sang "Oh, the picture of perfection! the joy unalloyed!"

But one cried of a sudden—"It seems that somewhere there is a break in the chain of light and one of the stars has been lost."

The golden string of their harp snapped, their song stopped, and they cried in dismay—"Yes, that lost star was the best, she was the glory of all heavens!"

From that day the search is unceasing for her, and the cry goes on from one to the other that in her the world has lost its one joy!

Only in the deepest silence of night the stars smile and whisper among themselves—"Vain is this seeking! unbroken perfection is over all!"

78

混沌初开，繁星初现，灿烂光辉，众神会集在天上唱着：“啊，完美的画图，纯粹的快乐！”

突然，一位神叫道——“光链有个地方似乎断了一环，一颗星星不见了。”

他们竖琴的金弦绷断，歌声停止了，他们沮丧地喊道——“对，那颗丢失的星星最美丽，她是诸天的荣光！”

从那天起，他们不停地寻找她，传遍众神的喊声都说世界因为她失去了一种喜悦。

只有在最深沉寂静的夜里，众星笑着互相低语说——“这寻找是多么徒劳啊！无破损的完美正笼罩着一切！”

假如此生注定我无缘遇见你，让我永远感到我错过与你见面。

If it is not my portion to meet thee in this life then let me ever feel that I have missed thy sight—let me not forget for a moment, let me carry the pangs of this sorrow in my dreams and in my wakeful hours.

As my days pass in the crowded market of this world and my hands grow full with the daily profits, let me ever feel that I have gained nothing—let me not forget for a moment, let me carry the pangs of this sorrow in my dreams and in my wakeful hours.

When I sit by the roadside, tired and panting, when I spread my bed low in the dust, let me ever feel that the long journey is still before me—let me not forget for a moment, let me carry the pangs of this sorrow in my dreams and in my wakeful hours.

When my rooms have been decked out and the flutes sound and the laughter there is loud, let me ever feel that I have not invited thee to my house—let me not forget for a moment, let me carry the pangs of this sorrow in my dreams and in my wakeful hours.

79

假如此生注定我无缘遇见你，让我永远感到我错过与你见面——让我一刻也不忘，让我梦里、醒时都带着这悔恨的痛楚。

当我在今世闹市中度日，手中赚满每日的赢利时，让我永远感到一无所获——让我一刻也不忘，让我梦里、醒时都带着这悔恨的痛楚。

当我坐在路边，疲惫喘息时，当我在尘土中铺下卧具时，让我永远感到前路依然漫长——让我一刻也不忘，让我梦里、醒时都带着这悔恨的痛楚。

当我的房间装饰好了，笛声响起，欢笑声朗朗时，让我永远感到我还没有邀请你到我的屋子——让我一刻也不忘，让我梦里、醒时都带着这悔恨的痛楚。

像一片秋日残云，我徒劳地飘荡在天空，啊，我永远壮丽的太阳！

I am like a remnant of a cloud of autumn uselessly roaming in the sky. O my sun ever-glorious! Thy touch has not yet melted my vapour, making me one with thy light, and thus I count months and years separated from thee.

If this be thy wish and if this be thy play, then take this fleeting emptiness of mine, paint it with colours, gild it with gold, float it on the wanton wind and spread it in varied wonders.

And again when it shall be thy wish to end this play at night, I shall melt and vanish away in the dark, or it may be in a smile of the white morning, in a coolness of purity transparent.

80

像一片秋日残云，我徒劳地飘荡在天空，啊，我永远壮丽的太阳！你的轻抚还没有消散我的水汽，使我与你的光明合一，因此我数着和你分离的年月。

假如这是你的意愿，假如这是你的游戏，那就把我这飞逝的空虚拿去吧，给它涂上颜色，镀上金光，让它飘浮在变幻不定的风中，舒卷成各种奇观。

假如你还愿意在夜间结束这场游戏，我将融化、消逝在黑暗中，或在洁白清晨的微笑中，在透明纯净的清凉中。

隐藏在万物心里，你滋养种子发芽，
蓓蕾成花朵，花朵成果实。

On many an idle day have I grieved over lost time. But it is never lost, my lord. Thou hast taken every moment of my life in thine own hands.

Hidden in the heart of things thou art nourishing seeds into sprouts, buds into blossoms, and ripening flowers into fruitfulness.

I was tired and sleeping on my idle bed and imagined all work had ceased. In the morning I woke up and found my garden full with wonders of flowers.

81

许多懒散的日子，我痛惜光阴虚度。但光阴绝不会虚度，我的上主。你手中掌管着我生命的分秒。

隐藏在万物心里，你滋养种子发芽，蓓蕾成花朵，花朵成果实。

我累了，睡在休闲的床榻上，想象着一切劳作已终了。清晨醒来，我发现园中鲜花遍开的奇景。

日夜更替，时代像花开花落。你知道如何去等待。

Time is endless in thy hands, my lord. There is none to count thy minutes.

Days and nights pass and ages bloom and fade like flowers. Thou knowest how to wait.

Thy centuries follow each other perfecting a small wild flower.

We have no time to lose, and having no time we must scramble for our chances. We are too poor to be late.

And thus it is that time goes by while I give it to every querulous man who claims it, and thine altar is empty of all offerings to the last.

At the end of the day I hasten in fear lest thy gate be shut; but I find that yet there is time.

82

你手中的光阴无限，我的主。你的分秒无法计算。

日夜更替，时代像花开花落。你知道如何去等待。

你的世纪接踵而至，只为了使一朵小野花尽善尽美。

我们没时间可浪费，只因没有时间，我们必须争取机会。我们太穷了，不能迟到。

就这样光阴消逝，我把时间给了每位牢骚满腹向我索取它的人，直到最后，你的神坛空空，没有任何祭品。

白日将尽，我赶忙前来，生怕你的门就要关上；而我发现时间还充裕。

母亲，我要用悲痛的泪水串成珠链挂在你的颈上。

Mother, I shall weave a chain of pearls for thy neck with my tears of sorrow.

The stars have wrought their anklets of light to deck thy feet, but mine will hang upon thy breast.

Wealth and fame come from thee and it is for thee to give or to withhold them. But this my sorrow is absolutely mine own, and when I bring it to thee as my offering thou rewardest me with thy grace.

83

母亲，我要用悲痛的泪水串成珠链挂在你的颈上。

星星把光明做成脚镯来装饰你的双脚，但我的珠链要挂在你胸前。

财富和声名来自你，施予或拒绝取决于你。但这悲痛完全属于我自己，当我把它当成祭品献给你时，你就用你的慈恩奖赏我。

这别离的悲痛，整夜沉默地望着星辰，在七月多雨的黑暗中，变成抒情诗，汇入树叶沙沙的声响。

It is the pang of separation that spreads throughout the world and gives birth to shapes innumerable in the infinite sky.

It is this sorrow of separation that gazes in silence all nights from star to star and becomes lyric among rustling leaves in rainy darkness of July.

It is this overspreading pain that deepens into loves and desires, into sufferings and joy in human homes; and this it is that ever melts and flows in songs through my poet's heart.

84

这别离的痛苦弥漫世界，在无垠的天空生出无数形态。

这别离的悲痛，整夜沉默地望着星辰，在七月多雨的黑暗中，变成抒情诗，汇入树叶沙沙的声响。

这蔓延的痛苦变得深重，成为爱和欲望，成为人们家庭的苦难和喜悦；它永远通过诗人的心，融化、流淌成诗歌。

他们放下刀剑和弓箭；和平在他们额上。

When the warriors came out first from their master's hall, where had they hid their power? Where were their armour and their arms?

They looked poor and helpless, and the arrows were showered upon them on the day they came out from their master's hall.

When the warriors marched back again to their master's hall where did they hide their power?

They had dropped the sword and dropped the bow and the arrow; peace was on their foreheads, and they had left the fruits of their life behind them on the day they marched back again to their master's hall.

85

当勇士们刚从他们主人的厅堂走出时，他们把威武藏在何处？他们的盔甲和兵器在哪里？

他们显得无助、可怜，当他们从他们主人的厅堂走出的那一天，箭如雨点飞向他们。

当勇士们列队走回他们主人的厅堂时，他们把威武藏在何处？

他们放下刀剑和弓箭；和平在他们额上，当他们列队走回他们主人的厅堂那一天，他们把生命的果实留在身后了。

夜色深沉，我心里害怕——但我要拿起灯，打开门，俯首恭迎他。

Death, thy servant, is at my door. He has crossed the unknown sea and brought thy call to my home.

The night is dark and my heart is fearful—yet I will take up the lamp, open my gates and bow to him my welcome. It is thy messenger who stands at my door.

I will worship him with folded hands, and with tears. I will worship him placing at his feet the treasure of my heart.

He will go back with his errand done, leaving a dark shadow on my morning; and in my desolate home only my forlorn self will remain as my last offering to thee.

86

死亡，你的仆人，正在我的门前。他涉过不可知的海把你的诏令带到我的家。

夜色深沉，我心里害怕——但我要拿起灯，打开门，俯首恭迎他。因为站在我门前的是你的使者。

我要敬拜他，双手合十，带着泪水。我要敬拜他，把我心中的珍宝放在他的脚前。

他完成了差事就要回去，给我的清晨留下黑影；只有我孤凄的自我留在我荒凉的家，作为最后的祭品献给你。

站在你夜空金色的天篷下，我抬起热切的眼睛仰望着你的脸。

In desperate hope I go and search for her in all the corners of my room; I find her not.

My house is small and what once has gone from it can never be regained.

But infinite is thy mansion, my lord, and seeking her I have to come to thy door.

I stand under the golden canopy of thine evening sky and I lift my eager eyes to thy face.

I have come to the brink of eternity from which nothing can vanish—no hope, no happiness, no vision of a face seen through tears.

Oh, dip my emptied life into that ocean, plunge it into the deepest fullness. Let me for once feel that lost sweet touch in the allness of the universe.

87

在急切的希望中，我到房间里各个角落寻找她；可我找不到她。

我的屋子很小，一旦从中丢失东西就永远不可复得。

可你的府第无边无际，我的主，为了寻找她，我不得不来到你的门前。

站在你夜空金色的天篷下，我抬起热切的眼睛仰望着你的脸。

我来到永恒的边缘，万物都不会从那里消失——希望、幸福或是穿过泪眼望见的一张模糊的脸。

啊，把我空虚的生命浸没在这海洋里，把它投入到这至深的圆满里吧。让我在宇宙的完整里，再一次感觉那失去的甜美爱抚吧。

许多节庆日子，你都在沉寂中度过，
荒废殿宇里的神啊。许多朝拜之夜在
灯火未燃中逝去。

Deity of the ruined temple! The broken strings of *Vina* sing no more your praise. The bells in the evening proclaim not your time of worship. The air is still and silent about you.

In your desolate dwelling comes the vagrant spring breeze. It brings the tidings of flowers—the flowers that for your worship are offered no more.

Your worshipper of old wanders ever longing for favour still refused. In the eventide, when fires and shadows mingle with the gloom of dust, he wearily comes back to the ruined temple with hunger in his heart.

Many a festival day comes to you in silence, deity of the ruined temple. Many a night of worship goes away with lamp unlit.

Many new images are built by masters of cunning art and carried to the holy stream of oblivion when their time is come.

Only the deity of the ruined temple remains unworshipped in deathless neglect.

88

荒废殿宇里的神啊！七弦琴的断弦不再弹唱赞美你的歌。晚钟不再宣告朝拜你的时辰。你四周的空气寂静无声。

游荡的春风来到你荒凉的居所。它带来了花儿的信息——可再也没人敬献鲜花来朝拜你。

你过去的朝拜者永远徘徊迷惑，企盼那还被拒施的恩典。日暮时分，光影交杂在尘埃的朦胧中，他带着饥饿的心，疲惫地回到这荒废的殿宇。

许多节庆日子，你都在沉寂中度过，荒废殿宇里的神啊。许多朝拜之夜在灯火未燃中逝去。

能工巧匠塑造了许多新的神像，当大限到来时，它们就被抬走抛入遗忘的圣河里。

只有荒废殿宇里的神永远无人朝拜，永远受人忽视。

那就让花儿在我园中开放，虽然花期未至；就让正午蜜蜂发出它们懒散的嗡嗡声吧。

No more noisy, loud words from me—such is my master's will. Henceforth I deal in whispers. The speech of my heart will be carried on in murmurings of a song.

Men hasten to the King's market. All the buyers and sellers are there. But I have my untimely leave in the middle of the day, in the thick of work.

Let then the flowers come out in my garden, though it is not their time; and let the midday bees strike up their lazy hum.

Full many an hour have I spent in the strife of the good and the evil, but now it is the pleasure of my playmate of the empty days to draw my heart on to him; and I know not why is this sudden call to what useless inconsequence!

89

我不再吵闹，不再高谈阔论了——这是我主人的旨意。此后我将轻声细语。我将用歌曲呢喃唱出我心里的话语。

人们匆忙赶往国王的集市，所有做买卖的人都在那里。中午时分，活儿正繁忙时，我却提早离开了。

那就让花儿在我园中开放，虽然花期未至；就让正午蜜蜂发出它们懒散的嗡嗡声吧。

在善恶交战中，我费时颇多，但此时空虚的日子里，我的玩伴有兴致把我的心拉到他那里；我不知道这突然的召唤是为什么，会导致什么无益突兀的事情。

我要在客人面前摆上我满满的生命之杯——我决不让他空着手回去。

On the day when death will knock at thy door what wilt thou offer to him?

Oh, I will set before my guest the full vessel of my life—I will never let him go with empty hands.

All the sweet vintage of all my autumn days and summer nights, all the earnings and gleanings of my busy life will I place before him at the close of my days when death will knock at my door.

90

有一天，死神会敲响你的门，你用什么敬献给他呢?

啊，我要在客人面前摆上我满满的生命之杯——我决不让他空着手回去。

我所有秋日和夏夜一切香甜的佳酿，我忙碌生命中一切所得和收获，在我临终的日子，死神来敲门时，我都要摆在他面前。

你的眼睛最后一瞥，我的生命就永远是你的。花儿已经编成，花环为新郎准备好了。

O thou the last fulfilment of life, Death, my death, come and whisper to me!

Day after day I have kept watch for thee; for thee have I borne the joys and pangs of life.

All that I am, that I have, that I hope and all my love have ever flowed towards thee in depth of secrecy. One final glance from thine eyes and my life will be ever thine own.

The flowers have been woven and the garland is ready for the bridegroom. After the wedding the bride shall leave her home and meet her lord alone in the solitude of night.

91

啊，你这生命最后的满足，死亡，我的死亡，来吧，向我耳语吧！

我天天守候着你；为了你，我忍受着生命的苦痛和欢乐。

我所有的存在、拥有、希望和爱，一直在秘密的深处向你奔流。你的眼睛最后一瞥，我的生命就永远是你的。

花儿已经编成，花环为新郎准备好了。婚礼过后，新娘就要回家，在幽静的夜里和她的主人单独相会。

我徒然渴望的东西以及我所得到的东西——让它们消逝吧。

I know that the day will come when my sight of this earth shall be lost, and life will take its leave in silence, drawing the last curtain over my eyes.

Yet stars will watch at night, and morning rise as before, and hours heave like sea waves casting up pleasures and pains.

When I think of this end of my moments, the barrier of the moments breaks and I see by the light of death thy world with its careless treasures. Rare is its lowliest seat, rare is its meanest of lives.

Things that I longed for in vain and things that I got—let them pass. Let me but truly possess the things that I ever spurned and overlooked.

92

我知道这一天将要来临，这大地的景象会在我眼里消失，生命默默地向我道别，把最后的帷幕拉过我眼前。

然而，星辰仍在夜里守望，晨曦依旧升起，时光仍像海潮一样起伏，荡起欢乐和哀伤。

当我想到我临终时刻，时光片段的阻碍被打破，在死亡的光明中，我看到你的世界珍宝随意洒落。最低下的席位最稀奇，最下等的人最珍贵。

我徒然渴望的东西以及我所得到的东西——让它们消逝吧。只要让我真正拥有那些我一直蔑视和视而不见的东西。

我放弃对我房子的一切占有。我只要你们最后亲切的话语。

I have got my leave. Bid me farewell, my brothers! I bow to you all and take my departure.

Here I give back the keys of my door—and I give up all claims to my house. I only ask for last kind words from you.

We were neighbours for long, but I received more than I could give. Now the day has dawned and the lamp that lit my dark corner is out. A summons has come and I am ready for my journey.

93

我已获准离去。兄弟们，与我道别吧！我向大家鞠躬，然后启程离开。

在此我把房门的钥匙交还——我放弃对我房子的一切占有。我只要你们最后亲切的话语。

我们做了很久的邻居，可我接受的比我给予的多。现在天已破晓，照亮我黑暗屋角的灯已熄灭。诏令已到，我已做好了旅途的准备。

此刻我离去时，祝我好运吧，我的朋友！天空晨曦泛红，我眼前有美好的道路。

At this time of my parting, wish me good luck, my friends! The sky is flushed with the dawn and my path lies beautiful.

Ask not what I have with me to take there. I start on my journey with empty hands and expectant heart.

I shall put on my wedding garland. Mine is not the red-brown dress of the traveller, and though there are dangers on the way I have no fear in mind.

The evening star will come out when my voyage is done and the plaintive notes of the twilight melodies be struck up from the King's gateway.

94

此刻我离去时，祝我好运吧，我的朋友！天空晨曦泛红，我眼前有美好的道路。

不要问我要带些什么到那边。带着期待的心，我两手空空踏上行程。

我要戴上我婚礼的花环。我不穿旅人红褐色的行装，虽然路上有险阻，我心里没有恐惧。

我的旅途尽时晚星将升起，黄昏乐曲哀婉的音符从王宫的入口奏起。

是什么力量使我向这浩瀚的神秘开放，像夜半林中一朵花蕾！

I was not aware of the moment when I first crossed the threshold of this life.

What was the power that made me open out into this vast mystery like a bud in the forest at midnight!

When in the morning I looked upon the light I felt in a moment that I was no stranger in this world, that the inscrutable without name and form had taken me in its arms in the form of my own mother.

Even so, in death the same unknown will appear as ever known to me. And because I love this life, I know I shall love death as well.

The child cries out when from the right breast the mother takes it away, in the very next moment to find in the left one its consolation.

95

当我刚刚跨过此生的门坎时，我并没觉察到那瞬间。

是什么力量使我向这浩瀚的神秘开放，像夜半林中一朵花蕾！

早晨我看到那光明时，我即刻感到我不是这个世界的陌生人，那无名无形不可思议者，以我母亲的形象把我拥在它的臂弯里。

甚至，在死亡里，那同一个不可知者又以我一向可知者出现。因为我爱此生，我知道我也会爱死亡。

当母亲把婴儿从右乳移开时，他就啼哭，紧接着他又从左乳找到安慰。

我曾经品尝过开在光明之海的莲花里隐藏的花蜜，因此我受到了祝福。

When I go from hence let this be my parting word, that what I have seen is unsurpassable.

I have tasted of the hidden honey of this lotus that expands on the ocean of light, and thus am I blessed—let this be my parting word.

In this playhouse of infinite forms I have had my play and here have I caught sight of him that is formless.

My whole body and my limbs have thrilled with his touch who is beyond touch; and if the end comes here, let it come—let this be my parting word.

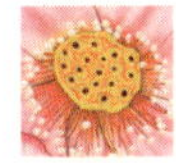

96

当我离开此处时，就用这作为我临别的话语吧，就说我所见过的无与伦比。

我曾经品尝过开在光明之海的莲花里隐藏的花蜜，因此我受到了祝福——就让这作为我临别的话语吧。

在这形态无数的游戏室里，我已玩过了，在这里我也瞥见了那无形的他。

他那无与伦比的爱抚使我浑身上下颤栗；如果死亡来到这里，让它来吧——就让这作为我临别的话语吧。

世界垂下眼睛看着你的双脚，和静默群星一道敬畏地站着。

When my play was with thee I never questioned who thou wert. I knew nor shyness nor fear, my life was boisterous.

In the early morning thou wouldst call me from my sleep like my own comrade and lead me running from glade to glade.

On those days I never cared to know the meaning of songs thou sangest to me. Only my voice took up the tunes, and my heart danced in their cadence.

Now, when the playtime is over, what is this sudden sight that is come upon me? The world with eyes bent upon thy feet stands in awe with all its silent stars.

97

当我与你玩耍时，我从不问起你是谁。我既不懂得羞怯，也不知道恐惧，我的生命兴高采烈。

像我自己的伙伴，大清早你把我从睡梦中叫醒，带我在林中空地之间奔跑。

那些日子，我从不在意去理解你为我唱的歌曲的含义。我只按调子发声，我的心随它们的节奏起舞。

现在，玩耍的时间已过，这突然降临在我眼前的景象是什么呢？世界垂下眼睛看着你的双脚，和静默群星一道敬畏地站着。

我将以战利品，我失败的花环，来装饰你。我永远没有力量逃脱、不被征服。

I will deck thee with trophies, garlands of my defeat. It is never in my power to escape unconquered.

I surely know my pride will go to the wall, my life will burst its bonds in exceeding pain, and my empty heart will sob out in music like a hollow reed, and the stone will melt in tears.

I surely know the hundred petals of a lotus will not remain closed for ever and the secret recess of its honey will be bared.

From the blue sky an eye shall gaze upon me and summon me in silence. Nothing will be left for me, nothing whatever, and utter death shall I receive at thy feet.

98

我将以战利品，我失败的花环，来装饰你。我永远没有力量逃脱、不被征服。

我确知我的骄傲会碰壁，我的生命会因为极度苦痛而挣脱束缚，我空虚的心会像空管芦笛呜咽着发出曲调，顽石也会熔化成泪水。

我确知百瓣莲花不会永远合着，它隐藏花蜜之处将显露。

碧空中有一只眼睛凝视着我，默默地召唤我。什么也不要留给我，无论什么也不要留，我将在你脚下接纳完全的死亡。

我这几盏灯被风儿轻轻一吹就熄灭了，为了重新燃起它们，我一再忘记所有别的事。

When I give up the helm I know that the time has come for thee to take it. What there is to do will be instantly done. Vain is this struggle.

Then take away your hands and silently put up with your defeat, my heart, and think it your good fortune to sit perfectly still where you are placed.

These my lamps are blown out at every little puff of wind, and trying to light them I forget all else again and again.

But I shall be wise this time and wait in the dark, spreading my mat on the floor; and whenever it is thy pleasure, my lord, come silently and take thy seat here.

99

当我放下舵轮时，我知道该是由你接过的时候了。该做的事顷刻就会做好，这挣扎是徒劳的。

那就把你的手拿开，默默地忍受失败吧，我的心啊，想想你被安置在一处，安然静坐的好运吧。

我这几盏灯被风儿轻轻一吹就熄灭了，为了重新燃起它们，我一再忘记所有别的事。

可这次我要聪明些，在黑暗中等待，把我的垫子铺在地上；无论何时你有兴致，我的主，悄悄地来此就坐吧。

我要带着我生命的竖琴走进那无底深渊旁的大殿，那里，音乐从无调之弦生起。

I dive down into the depth of the ocean of forms, hoping to gain the perfect pearl of the formless.

No more sailing from harbour to harbour with this my weather-beaten boat. The days are long passed when my sport was to be tossed on waves.

And now I am eager to die into the deathless.

Into the audience hall by the fathomless abyss where swells up the music of toneless strings I shall take this harp of my life.

I shall tune it to the notes of forever, and when it has sobbed out its last utterance, lay down my silent harp at the feet of the silent.

100

我潜入形体之海的深处，希望得到那无形完美的珍珠。

我饱经风雨之舟不再驶往一个个海港，我乐于在波涛上颠簸的日子早已过去。

现在我渴望死去，进入那无死之境。

我要带着我生命的竖琴走进那无底深渊旁的大殿，那里，音乐从无调之弦生起。

我要调理琴弦应和那永恒的音符，当它呜咽着发出最后声响时，我就把我沉寂的竖琴放在寂静者的脚边。

这一生，我永远以歌曲来寻找你。它们把我心里天空的许多星辰带到我眼前。

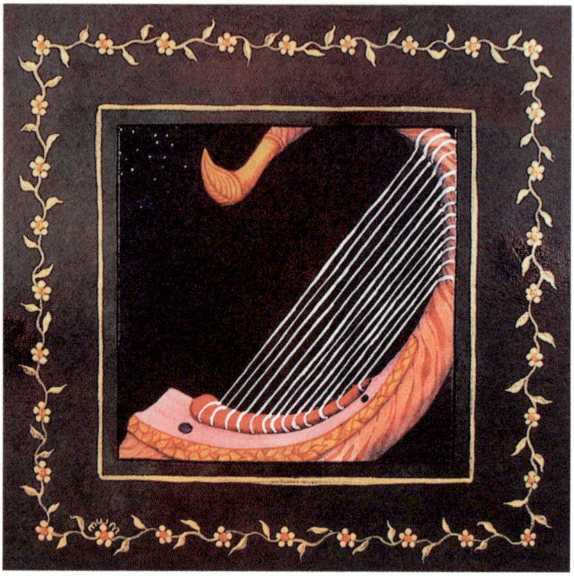

Ever in my life have I sought thee with my songs. It was they who led me from door to door, and with them have I felt about me, searching and touching my world.

It was my songs that taught me all the lessons I ever learnt; they showed me secret paths, they brought before my sight many a star on the horizon of my heart.

They guided me all the day long to the mysteries of the country of pleasure and pain, and, at last, to what palace gate have they brought me in the evening at the end of my journey?

101

这一生，我永远以歌曲来寻找你。是它们带我走家串户，我用它们感知自己、求索和触及我的世界。

我所学的功课都是我的歌曲教给我的；它们向我展示秘密路径，它们把我心里天空的许多星辰带到我眼前。

它们整天把我带到痛苦和快乐的神秘疆域，最后，在我旅程结束的黄昏，它们会把我带到哪座宫殿的门口呢?

我把你的传说谱写成恒久的歌。那秘密从我心中迸发。

I boasted among men that I had known you. They see your pictures in all works of mine. They come and ask me, "Who is he?" I know not how to answer them. I say, "Indeed, I cannot tell." They blame me and they go away in scorn. And you sit there smiling.

I put my tales of you into lasting songs. The secret gushes out from my heart. They come and ask me, "Tell me all your meanings." I know not how to answer them. I say, "Ah, who knows what they mean!" They smile and go away in utter scorn. And you sit there smiling.

102

我在人前夸口说我认识你。他们见到你的形象在我所有的作品中，他们来问我："他是谁?"我不知如何作答。我说："其实，我也说不出。"他们责备我，鄙夷地走开。你却坐在那里微微笑。

我把你的传说谱写成恒久的歌。那秘密从我心中迸发。他们来问我："告诉我们所有的意思吧。"我不知如何作答。我说："啊，谁知道那些歌曲是什么意思!"他们笑了，极端鄙夷地走开。你却坐在那里微微笑。

像一群思归的鹤鸟，日夜飞回它们的高山之巢，让我整个生命启程回到它永恒的家园。

In one salutation to thee, my God, let all my senses spread out and touch this world at thy feet.

Like a rain-cloud of July hung low with its burden of unshed showers let all my mind bend down at thy door in one salutation to thee.

Let all my songs gather together their diverse strains into a single current and flow to a sea of silence in one salutation to thee.

Like a flock of homesick cranes flying night and day back to their mountain nests let all my life take its voyage to its eternal home in one salutation to thee.

103

在一次对你的敬拜中，我的上主，让我展开所有的感觉，触及你脚下的世界。

在一次对你的敬拜中，像七月积雨云低垂，带着未下阵雨的重负，让我全心俯首在你门前。

在一次对你的敬拜中，让我的所有歌曲，聚集不同旋律，形成一股洪流，注入寂静的大海。

在一次对你的敬拜中，像一群思归的鹤鸟，日夜飞回它们的高山之巢，让我整个生命启程回到它永恒的家园。

附录：泰戈尔和《吉檀迦利》

一、诺贝尔奖

在西方人看来，1913年，不知从何处冒出一位名叫罗宾德拉纳特·泰戈尔（Rabindranath Tagore）的人，毫不费劲地拿走了诺贝尔文学奖，然后周游世界，受到世人景仰长达二十多年，二十世纪任何作家都不曾有此殊荣。泰戈尔像一阵旋风席卷了世界文坛，波及了当时几乎所有大文豪和各界名流，有的狂热，有的冷静。叶芝（W. B. Yeats）对泰戈尔诗歌的热情持续了很久，庞德（Ezra Pound）在他的《吉檀迦利》长篇评论中，把他与但丁相提并论。

1913年11月14日下午，在自己创立的学校，泰戈尔得知他获得诺贝尔文学奖的消息。恰巧爱德华·汤姆森（Edward Thompson），即后来泰戈尔的传记作家，首次访问那所学校，记录了泰戈尔对这一惊人消息的反应：

> 孩子们疯狂了。他们不知道什么是诺贝尔奖，但他们知道他们敬爱的老师做了一件了不起的事。他们排成队伍走过老师住处，唱着校歌……他出来了，然后他们被一阵狂热的崇拜所控制，一个接一个下跪，触到他的双脚。那位被尊为圣人的人站着，感到不自在，用双手抚住脸，请求宽恕。

诺贝尔奖委员会对《吉檀迦利》中，哪些是泰戈尔原创，哪些是他对印度传统中奉爱诗歌的模仿有疑问。可是，有一点毫无疑问，《吉檀迦利》表达了理想主义，这一点极为重要。许多委员会成员非常推崇《吉檀迦利》。瑞典诗人魏尔纳·冯·海登斯塔姆(Verner von Heidenstam，1916年诺贝尔文学奖得主)的观点对泰戈尔获奖至关重要。他写道：

> 正像歌德诗选使我们相信他的伟大一样，即便我们不熟悉他的其他作品，对泰戈尔的这些作品，我们也完全可以这么说……我带着强烈的情感阅读了这些诗歌，可以说过去几十年里，在诗歌文学方面，我从未遇到过同样的作品。这些诗歌给我带来特别的时光，我好像喝到清泉活水。爱和强烈的宗教感渗透了他所有思想和感情，心地纯洁，高贵而不造作，形成了一个深刻、稀有的灵性之美的总体印象。没有令人争议，令人不安，没有空虚、世俗、琐碎的东西，如果说有人具备获诺贝尔奖的特质，那就是泰戈尔。据我所知，没有任何其他活着的诗人能与他媲美。

1913年，泰戈尔“由于他那至为敏锐、清新而优美的诗篇；这些诗篇不但具有高超的技巧，而且由他自己用英文表达出来，使他那充满诗意的思想成为西方文学的一部分”而荣膺诺贝尔文学奖，成为亚洲第一位获此殊荣的作家。由于路途遥远，他未能亲临颁奖典礼。他回电报说：“我恳切地向瑞典文学院表示对那博大理解的感谢与领受；这理解将远的拉近，也使陌生人成为兄弟。”

二、《吉檀迦利》的创作背景

泰戈尔的孟加拉语诗集《吉檀迦利》，出版于1910年，共有 157 首诗。英文版《吉檀迦利》（*Gitanjali* 或者 *Song Offerings*）有 103 首诗歌，是泰戈尔 1912 年去英国前不久翻译的，其中 53 首译自原版孟加拉语《吉檀迦利》，其余 50 首是分别从他的一部戏剧和其他 8 部诗集中选译的。在泰戈尔六十多年的创作生涯中，产出和题材多样都令人惊叹，孟加拉语作品有 26 大卷，包括诗歌、戏剧、歌剧、短篇小说、长篇小说、散文和日记等，还有二十多卷信件。他还创作了两千五百多首歌曲，两千多幅油画和素描。在孟加拉国，这些著作中的大部分仍然有人阅读、演出和研究。《吉檀迦利》是他毕生创作中最重要的一部诗集。

1905 年，孟加拉刮起了爱国情感的风暴：我们的祖国运动（The Swadeshi Movement，英文意为 Our Country Movement）。当时英国在印度的统治难以为继。1904 年，为了在印度制造矛盾，分而治之，英国印度总督柯曾勋爵（Lord Curzon）将孟加拉东西分治。《分治法案》激起的这场爱国运动，强调印度教徒和穆斯林教徒的团结，波及了泰戈尔。他创作了许多爱国歌曲，广为传唱，有两首歌后来分别成为孟加拉国和印度的国歌。泰戈尔是运动的主要成员之一。由于孟加拉没有人愿意当领导人，泰戈尔成为唯一适合的人选。当这个职务落在他身上时，他觉得没法承担，退避到桑提尼克坦。他对爱国运动感兴趣在于国民教育而不是政治，由于他的诗人气质，即便运动处于高潮，他也保持距离。后来，该运动出现了暴力抗英现象，更使他敬而远之。泰戈尔激发了这场运动，又远离了它，因此，很多热心运动的人也疏远了他。部分加尔各答的作家和记者，妒忌他家境富裕和文学成就，带着报复，加入了大众对他的指责。

这期间，在家庭中，泰戈尔接连遭受亲人去世的不幸。1902 年，他的妻子去世，年仅 30 岁。妻子死前不久，12 岁的二女儿瑞奴卡（Renuka）染上了肺结核，于1903年夭折。1905年，84岁的父亲去世。1907年，小儿子沙民德拉那特（Samindranath）死于霍乱。亲人的相继离世和爱国运动的失败，国人对他尖锐的批评日益增加，宗教正统对他的敌意上升，同时，他与到访印度的西方人交往频密，开始抛弃加在自己身上的狭隘的爱国主义的限制，等等，这一系列事，都促使他深入思考宗教、教育、社会和政治等方面。

这期间，泰戈尔发表了很多文章，但很少发表诗歌和小说。随后几年，在他1912年对西方的历史性访问之前，他在小说和诗歌方面创作颇丰，孟加拉语《吉檀迦利》就是创作于这一时期。从创作《吉檀迦利》的社会以及家庭背景我们可以看到，当时的社会困境以及家庭不幸对泰戈尔的影响深刻地反映在这部诗集中，许多篇章充满了对死亡的思考与超越。

三、《吉檀迦利》在西方的出版

英国画家威廉·罗森斯坦（William Rothenstein）通过泰戈尔的侄儿阿巴宁拉纳特（Abanindranath Tagore）认识了泰戈尔，对泰戈尔的形象和作品印象深刻。受罗森斯坦的盛情邀请，1911年10月，他准备和儿子儿媳一起访问英国，但是由于生病，直到1912年5月底才成行。英文《吉檀迦利》是泰戈尔在舍利达（Shelidah）养病期间翻译的。

1912年6月16日，泰戈尔一行刚抵达伦敦就把装有唯一《吉檀迦利》英文译稿的手提包遗失在地铁上。幸运的是，该火车站的失物招领处帮助他们找回。

最先读到手稿的是威廉·罗森斯坦，他欣喜若狂："这是一种新型的诗，神秘主义的杰作！"他赶紧联系诗人叶芝，还把泰戈尔介绍给英国作家、艺术家和思想家，并安排伦敦印度协会出版该诗集，由麦克米兰公司出版。他还照顾了泰戈尔一行的吃住。

7月27日，泰戈尔和叶芝第一次会面，在罗森斯坦家的黄昏聚会上，叶芝朗读了几首《吉檀迦利》中的诗篇。几天后的晚餐聚会，有七十多人参加，其中有叶芝的意中人莫德·冈恩（**Maud Gonne**）、作家H. G. 威尔斯（**H. G. Wells**）等。接下来大约一周内，叶芝忙于选择、编辑这些诗歌，并用铅笔标记，以便泰戈尔进一步修改。9月初，他写了序言让罗森斯坦过目，他这样写道：

> 我多日随身携带这些译文的手稿，在火车站、巴士上或在餐馆里阅读，我经常要把书稿合上，以免陌生人看到我多么受感动……
>
> 这些散文诗的译文……多年来从未有任何东西像这样使我热血沸腾……这些抒情诗……展现了我一生梦寐以求的世界。一种至高文明的产物，然而它们的出现却像小草生长在普普通通的土壤中。
>
> 要是孟加拉文明连续不断，要是那共同的心灵，像有人说的那样，流布一切，不像我们的，分裂成十几个互不相干的心灵，这些诗歌中最微妙的东西，在几代人后，甚至会使路边的乞讨者受益……
>
> 对于我们无限陌生的整个民族，整个文明，似乎开始了这种想象。我们并不为它的陌生而受感动，而是因为我们遇到了自己的形象，好像我们曾经走在罗塞蒂的柳树林中，或者，第一次在文学中听到我们梦境中的声音。

尽管对孟加拉诸多误解，这种热情具有强烈的感染力。10月2日，叶芝的朋友埃兹拉·庞德与泰戈尔共进晚餐，次日，整个下午与他讨论诗歌韵律，边看罗森斯坦为他画像，边听他朗诵和歌唱。麦克米兰出版公司于 1913 年 3 月出版了英文版《吉檀迦利》，同年 11 月 13 日，泰戈尔获得诺贝尔奖，在获得诺贝尔文学奖之前，该书重印了十次。

103 首诗歌中有些诗句被名人引用。第一次世界大战阵亡的英国著名诗人威尔弗雷德·欧文（Wilfred Owen）引用过第 96 首里的句子："当我离开此处时，就用这作为我临别的话语吧，就说我所见过的无与伦比。"庞德喜欢第 63 首里的句子，也是泰戈尔发电报致谢瑞典文学院引用的句子。叶芝在《吉檀迦利》的出版序言里引用第 60 首关于儿童的诗歌做结语。经常被引用的还有第 73 首里的句子："我不想了断尘缘寻求解脱。在无数快乐的束缚里我感到自由的拥抱。"圣雄甘地喜欢引用第 39 首里的句子："当我的心冷酷干枯时，请为我降下慈悲的甘霖。"整首经常被引用的有第 30 首，极具自传性的第 102 首，第 67 首被叶芝选为《牛津当代诗歌选集 1892—1935》中泰戈尔的七首诗歌之一。

《吉檀迦利》不可逆转地模塑了西方人脑海中泰戈尔的形象，一位灵秘诗人，来自东方的智者，"无为的梦想家，庄严而宁静"。爱德华·汤姆森认为，在他后来的翻译和他个人在西方的行为中，泰戈尔无疑推波助澜了这种印象。

泰戈尔的西方追随者看到，基督教仁爱精神理论上受尊敬，实践中受忽视，却以纯粹的形式，从《吉檀迦利》中映照到他们之中。泰戈尔的印度灵性观念和《新约》有着强烈的关联，他强调耶稣基督是东方人。达尔文的孙女弗兰西斯·科恩福德（Frances Cornford）告诉罗森斯坦："现在我能想象温和大能的耶稣了，之前我从来不能。"

泰戈尔一行在英国待了四个月，三个月在伦敦，一个月在乡间。10 月 19 日他们离开英国前往美国。

四、泰戈尔的成长经历

泰戈尔的祖父德瓦卡纳特·泰戈尔（Dwakanath Tagore）是一个非凡的人。当时，加尔各答是个仅次于伦敦的商业城市，他是那里首屈一指的商人、慈善家和企业家。在欧洲，他是“东方大富豪”，维多利亚女王的座上宾，被称为“德瓦卡纳特王子”。他在商业上精明，希望使印度工业化，他还是个文化名流。泰戈尔和他有许多类似之处，祖孙俩都喜欢音乐、戏曲和文学。二者都为人慷慨，喜欢旅游，经常住最好的宾馆，都好交往文人雅士，好与漂亮女性为伴，为祖国而感骄傲，相信西方的活力与法则，认为东西方应该合作，同时也都生活在矛盾中。

泰戈尔的父亲德本德拉纳特·泰戈尔（Debendranath Tagore）继承了家业，同时有超然、虔诚的信仰。他性格内省慎思，潜心于哲学和宗教著作研究，对艺术敏感，对实际工作精明善断。他温文尔雅、尊贵大方，博得了“玛哈希”（意为“大圣人”）的美称，对泰戈尔影响深远。

1861 年 5 月 7 日，在孟加拉国首都加尔各答，泰戈尔出生在德瓦卡纳特·泰戈尔街的一幢大楼里。母亲莎拉达（Sharada）已有 12 个孩子（7 个儿子，5 个女儿），其中几个已经有妻子或丈夫，住在同一幢楼里。

德本德拉纳特的子女都有充分自由，成长在虔诚的宗教气氛与美好的环境中。这个家庭继承了印度文化传统，又深受西方文化影响，常举行哲学和宗教讨论会、诗歌朗诵会，经常演戏，还安排音乐会。罗宾德拉纳特·泰戈尔就降生在这样的环境中，在他性格形成时期，“印度文艺复兴的急流从他的四周澎湃而过”。

他不喜欢学校，厌恶无视个性的教育制度，厌恶远离自然、牢笼般的教室，喜欢校外花园、池塘、春天和白云。他进过东方学院、师范学院和孟加拉国学院，但都没有完成学业。后来他创办学校，致力于教育革新与此有关。

8 岁左右他开始写诗，“像一只刚长角的小鹿到处跳来跳去，我和我诗歌的萌芽也讨厌地跳来跳去。”

1873 年对他很重要，父亲带着 12 岁的他去喜马拉雅山。他第一次到桑提尼克坦（Shantiniketan，意为平安之地，the Abode of Peace）。泰戈尔出生前不久，父亲在孟加拉国的贫困地区购置了这块荒地，这里成了泰戈尔脑海里的理想国。父子俩还来到锡克教寺院，临近现今巴基斯坦边界的旁遮普（Punjab），他的父亲加入唱祷。后来，泰戈尔一直把锡克教当成对印度教的改革运动、把佛教当成古代婆罗门教的改革运动，而不是分离的教派，他还推崇佛陀为有史以来最伟大的人。4 月中旬，旁遮普平原酷暑难当，他们带着仆人来到喜马拉雅山。当太阳从喜马拉雅山升起时，他们站立着颂唱《奥义书》，父亲鼓励儿子自我约束，发展独立精神，不要养成控制他人的行为习惯。

1936 年在桑提尼克坦，泰戈尔提到父亲，充满了感激和敬意：

> 那些日子父亲给我的印象是，作为担当一个大家庭责任的人，他总是使自己精神自由，不受凡俗事务羁绊，精神没有障碍，自由驰骋。当我想起父亲时，脑海里总是生起壮丽的喜马拉雅山干城章嘉峰（Kanchanjungha）的景象，一个无瑕遥远、辉煌的奇景，或者像《奥义书》中所说的那样：他站着，像一棵大树矗立在空中。

《奥义书》（*Upanishads*，印度教古代吠陀教义的思辨经典，为印度各派哲学的依据）里有句话对德本德拉纳特和泰戈尔本人以及甘地都有深刻影响，“无常世间万事皆变，须知万物都在他的包围下，他是万物之主。因此在舍弃中得到快乐吧，不要贪恋财富。”这种神显现在万物中的观念，在泰戈尔作品中反复出现，他尊《奥义书》为印度哲学的最高成就。但他发现：“在回答人类灵魂复杂的渴望方面，它不够完善。它太强调智慧，没有充分用爱和奉献的方式达到真谛。”

12 岁时他读了《罗摩衍那》（*Ramayana*，印度古代两大梵文史诗之一），匿名发表了第一首诗，题为《渴望》（*Yearning*）。拉比（泰戈尔的昵称）在家里接受宽松教育，文学是重要方面，他读梵文、英文和孟加拉文作品，也读但丁和歌德的英译本，但未读出趣味来。他阅读的英文著作还有拜伦的《哈雷德游记》（*Childe Harold's Pilgrimage*），穆尔的《爱尔兰小曲》（*Irish Melodies*），莎士比亚的《麦克白》和《暴风雨》等。

这期间，拉比和他的五哥乔蒂林德拉纳特（Jyotirindranath Tagore）最为亲近。五哥乔蒂是音乐家、戏剧家、诗人和新闻记者，长拉比 13 岁，对他十分赏识，从不强迫他做任何事，鼓励他阅读孟加拉国文学，并通过创办家庭文学杂志《婆罗蒂》月刊，直接引导他走上了文坛。后来他对兄长非正统的影响经常表示感激。

1875 年至 1876 年间，乔蒂带拉比走出加尔各答，到东孟加拉国泰戈尔家族的另一处房产，在舍利达，恒河的两条支流相汇处的一个村庄。在那里，他骑马、散步或骑大象去猎虎。当时他的文学偶像是比哈里拉尔·查克拉瓦提（Biharilal Chakravarti），一位四十多岁的诗人，以写优美抒情诗著称，拉比拜访他并听他朗读《罗摩衍那》和迦梨陀娑（Kalidasa）的作品《云使》等。

乔蒂林德拉纳特的妻子卡丹巴丽·黛薇（Kadambari Devi）丰姿绰约、优雅宽厚，她给拉比布置了优雅的环境，在他身上倾注了深深的爱。她成了拉比理想中的人物，两人之间有一种罗曼蒂克的眷恋。拉比在这样的家庭氛围里度过一生中最愉快的日子。嫂子的年龄与他相仿，欣赏他的诗，也非常欣赏比哈里拉尔·查克拉瓦提的诗。为了不使他虚荣心增长，她装作不欣赏他的诗歌和长相，不鼓励任何接触。

七十年代，一种相爱，半玩笑，天真的关系在他们之间产生。卡丹巴丽孩子气很浓，有孤独感，而拉比是个善感诗人的苗子。1875 年，他的母亲去世后，卡丹巴丽成了对少年泰戈尔影响最深的女人。

80 岁时，他温情地回忆道："当时没有电风扇，我读书时，我分享嫂子扇子的好处。"拉比称卡丹巴丽为赫卡特（Hecate，希腊神话中夜和冥界的女神），她回赠他一个名字巴奴（Bhanu，意为太阳）。1877 年，他的第一本诗集出版，就用 Bhanu Singh 做笔名。

1884 年 2 月，拉比婚前的诗集《画与歌》发表，献给卡丹巴丽。其中有一首诗题为《拉杜之爱》（*The Love of Radu*）。拉杜是印度神话里众所熟知的魔，一个无形的星体，爱上了月亮，永远追求她，有时把她吞噬，形成月食，明显暗示了爱欲。

诗集发表后两个月，嫂子卡丹巴丽自杀了，25 岁。一个女人生活在父权社会中，又不是一个文人，她情感的出口被堵塞了。拉比婚后，身体和精神上离开她的圈子对她是个重大打击。她的丈夫从事商业冒险蒙受重大损失。她喜欢阅读诗歌和小说，正统人认为这不适合女人，甚至会影响家庭和谐。公公的批评导致她思想失衡，加之她又是个不育的女人，1884 年 4 月 19 日，她服鸦片过量中毒而死。

1875 年，母亲的去世没有让拉比长久地悲伤，但卡丹巴丽是他第一个深爱的女人，她的死带给拉比的悲伤萦回不去。从那时起，死亡经常是他的伴侣，可以说，泰戈尔深刻思考死亡和卡丹巴丽的离世不无关系。《吉檀迦利》后面一些篇章表达了与死亡或神的使者和解的退隐情绪。

卡丹巴丽生前，泰戈尔有四本诗集献给她，死后，至少有两本书献给她。他在诗中写她，画中画她，一个神秘女人的脸孔时常出现。在他的歌曲中，她的影子挥之不去。她的死亡无疑使泰戈尔的作品更为深刻。晚年，他在回忆录中写道："自然之美在我的泪眼前呈现更深刻的意义。卡丹巴丽的逝去将我推到必要的距离，从整体上来看待诗、人生和世界。"

五、泰戈尔的婚姻和子女

泰戈尔在《我的回忆》中，从未提及他的妻子，只写道："我结婚了。"直至今天，知名印度人很少在书面上谈及自己的妻子。至于泰戈尔，一个几乎打破所有文学常规的人，有必要解释一下。

1878 年，泰戈尔的父亲决定让他去英国学习法律，希望他成为律师。在那里，他没有学成法律，倒是迷住了不少女孩子。他的长相令许多人倾倒。英驻德大使觉得他的长相比大多数西方人脑海中的耶稣还完美。但泰戈尔为西方女人的自由与精力充沛所吸引，同时也感到害怕。卖弄风情和对外表的痴迷对他没有吸引力。

在印度包办婚姻制度下，在子女的婚姻中，爱情的因素次要。1883 年 12 月 9 日，22 岁的拉比尊父命与一个名叫巴哈塔瑞妮（Bhahatarini），大约 10 岁的女孩子结婚。当时印度盛行女童婚制，通常男方是成年人，而女方只有 10 至 15 岁。

新娘体瘦，长相不佳，几乎没受过教育，他未和她见过面就接受了。新娘名字显得俗气，后来改为穆里娜莉妮（Mrinalini），意为莲花般的。泰戈尔对这位 10 岁的陌生人有何反应，鲜为人知。婚后一年，他和妻子还是完全分居。一方面，泰戈尔必须和他所有哥哥一样遵循家庭传统；另一方面，他可能觉得妻子和他理想中的人有差距。他对嫂子有过很深的依恋，也见识过西方姑娘。他保持沉默，或许说明他无法摆脱内心的冲突。

泰戈尔第一个孩子，女儿玛德胡瑞拉塔（Madhurilata），昵称为贝拉（Bela），生于 1886 年，当年他的妻子 13 岁，此后又生二女二男。1887 年，他做了关于印度婚姻制度的演讲，对自己的婚姻充满矛盾，该演讲理性、温和，谨慎地呼吁废止女童婚制，比一般孟加拉国受教育的人早几十年有这种想法。他认为大家族制和女童婚制压抑了人性发展。

泰戈尔用自己的诗歌教子女学孟加拉语，逐句逐字分析，但从不提语法，甚至让他的侄儿和受教育不久的妻子分别改写印度两大史诗《摩诃婆罗多》（*Mahabharata*）和《罗摩衍那》作为孩子们的读物。

在舍利达，有条恒河的支流叫帕德玛（Padma）。他和大儿子坐在自己家船的船沿上，突然儿子穿在脚上的拖鞋掉进河里，他不假思索地纵身跃入河中，和激流搏斗，捡回了拖鞋。有一次，他和他的穆斯林厨师撑着小船，从激流中救起了投河自尽的女子。盛年的泰戈尔为自己能游过帕德玛河颇感骄傲。他对子女不仅言传而且身教，船与帕德玛河对他和孩子们影响深远，晚年他在一首诗中回忆道：

我曾经住在她沙滩上的停泊处，
与世隔绝，远离人群。
清晨散步我看到启明星，

夜晚我睡在船顶上，
北斗星看顾着我。
我孤寂日子的联翩浮想
合入她远处激流的边缘，
像一个旅人走过。
家庭幸福和烦恼，既近又远。

四十岁中年将至，他越来越想移居到桑提尼克坦，到那“森林中隐居处”建一所学校。1901年，他先后把两个女儿嫁出去，大女儿贝拉不到15岁，二女儿瑞奴卡年仅10岁半，她们婚前从未见过她们要嫁的男人。他曾写信安慰妻子：“我们的家庭教育、趣味、传统、说话和思维方式跟其他孟加拉国家庭不一样，这就更有必要让我们的女儿在婚后远离我们……她们不是为我们的幸福而生的，我们的幸福在于为她们着想，使她们实现人生价值……”

这和他之前反对女童婚制相冲突，他这样做，最可能的动机是，当时他有一个无法抗拒的冲动就是要在桑提尼克坦办学校。爱国也好，自我中心也好，他听从了命运的召唤，觉得必须摆脱其他责任，比如对女儿的责任。他尽量使自己相信他是为了女儿好（晚年，他曾流露出对三个女儿婚事的内疚）。

1902年，妻子去世，此后几年，儿女、父亲和小儿子相继去世，给泰戈尔带来沉重打击。在《吉檀迦利》中有几篇深切表达了他对孩子们的爱，参看第60，61和62篇。

六、泰戈尔的诗歌传承

泰戈尔的诗歌，意象丰富，宗教感强，充满了对自然和祖国的热爱。毫无疑问，印度教的精神传统，尤其对毗湿奴的信仰是《吉檀迦利》意象之源，这使1912年的叶芝深受感动。印度教十一到十七世纪的“虔信派运动”（Bhakti Movement），尤其对三大主神之一毗湿奴的化身神克里希那（Krishna）的奉爱，激发了印度诗人通过情爱语言表达与神相融的诗歌。这种《旧约圣经》里《雅歌》式的情爱表达，使西方读者产生了广泛共鸣。身体的激情，感性的意象及语言的音乐性使《吉檀迦利》在世界文学中无与伦比。印度人善于表达爱和伤感。可以说，情感主义主导了孟加拉国人的生活，这使泰戈尔对英国文学中的激情很敏感,较少注意其理性的一面。早年泰戈尔曾说：

我们的文学之神是莎士比亚，弥尔顿和拜伦。他们的作品最感动我们的是激情的力量。英国社会生活中，激情的发泄受到严格约束。也许正是因为如此，激情主导了英国文学。其特点是把激情压抑到不可避免地爆发的边缘。至少我们孟加拉国人认为这是英国文学的本质。

英国文学中，后三位浪漫派诗人拜伦、雪莱和济慈对他影响深刻。在他的诗歌中，西方的激情与印度人的平静、善感和虔诚产生了微妙结合。1890年12月,他发表了诗集《意中女》（*Manashi*，意为 the Lady of Mind），主题是自然与爱，有些诗歌是对已故嫂子的追忆。诗集题目 Manashi 模糊得恰到好处，“脑海里生成的幻象”和“某人幻想的心上人”，也是孟加拉国女性的常用名。该诗集标志着泰戈尔已经成为能把握多种情绪的诗人，从柔情到辛辣讽刺。有个朋友觉察到他的诗中有“绝望和退隐情绪”。泰戈尔坦白的回答，道出他一生创作的轨迹：

有时我发现自己内心是两股相反的力量不断冲突的战场，一股把我引向和平，熄灭所有争吵，另一股怂恿我去战斗。似乎西方躁动不安的能量和行动的意志永无止境地攻击着我印度人平静的堡垒。……这种持续战斗带来了一系列复杂不安定的退隐情绪。

七、泰戈尔的理想和良知

为了将古老的印度精神和现代西方精神相结合，1901年，在加尔各答西北约100英里处的桑提尼克坦一块荒地上，他建起一所学校，20年后，在附近村庄，他建起了一所国际大学（Visva-Bharati）。在他的管理下，学校取得了很大成就，尤其在音乐、绘画、东方语言研究及乡村发展人才等方面，培养出一些出类拔萃的人才，如赛亚吉·雷（Satyajit Ray，1921—1992，印度著名导演）和英迪拉·甘地（Indira Gandhi，印度历史上第一位女总理，印度开国总理贾瓦哈拉尔·尼赫鲁的女儿）。19岁在读的英迪拉在写给她父亲的信中谈到桑提尼克坦："那里的空气中，他的精神似乎跟随你到处盘旋、漫游，带着爱和深深的看顾，我感到这种精神深刻地影响了我的生命和思想。"

泰戈尔后半生致力于把自己的理想灌输给他的同胞，他的理想是民主、爱和崇尚自然。从1918年到他最后的日子，泰戈尔把他的大学像十字架一样背在肩上，为筹集办学经费耗尽心血，献出了一切，牺牲了他最大的愿望——一个诗人梦寐以求的独处，放下架子成了一个乞讨者。可是民主的理想与他的本性并不相符，他的气质是贵族的，甚至他和孟加拉国人的关系也时常紧张。其实，他的朋友很少，即使有也不是终生的，他的家庭生活悲剧重重也与他有关系。

1919 年 4 月 13 日在阿姆利则（Amristar），英国军人下令杀害了至少 379 名非暴力抵抗运动者，致使 2000 多人受伤。5 月 30 日，泰戈尔宣布放弃四年前英国王室授予他的骑士称号，成为第一个公开反对阿姆利则大屠杀的知名印度人。泰戈尔和甘地彼此相互尊重，1913 年，甘地尚未广为人知，泰戈尔就发贺电给他，对他在南非进行的反种族主义斗争表达敬意。两年后甘地派弟子到桑提尼克坦学习，接着又亲自造访。泰戈尔首次称甘地为“圣雄”（Mahatma），甘地则称泰戈尔为“伟大的卫士”（The Great Sentinel），印度荣誉的守护者，但是，两人的气质和观念极不相同。

二十年代，他以坚定的理性批评了甘地在不合作运动中过激的做法。虽然泰戈尔对现代文明、机器和城市持很大保留态度，但他到底还是接受了这些。甘地则对吸收西方的东西毫无兴趣，认为西方应该变得像古老的印度。有一次甘地要泰戈尔自己纺纱，以传统印度文明抵制英国的现代化。泰戈尔回答说：“我可以编织诗歌、歌曲和戏剧，但编织你宝贵的棉花，我只会弄得一团糟。”

作为理想主义者，他对西方人文精神一直充满向往，最早接触到的是十九世纪英国文学和政治自由主义。直至 1920 年，他一直相信英国人对印度的统治是恰当的，对一个死气沉沉、退化的社会改革是必需的。但作为爱国主义者，尤其在 1900 年后，他相信古老印度的精神需要得到延续。在国外，他觉得有必要为印度精神辩护，但在印度，他赞誉西方精神。泰戈尔孟加拉国的一面，安宁、平静和满足，但他欧洲的一面渴望与艺术家、思想家和行动家接触。从本质上说，泰戈尔对政治不感兴趣。对他而言，教育失策是导致印度问题重重的主要原因。他痛恨教育体系单调，与生命和自然隔离，功利主义，对英语的强调几乎挤掉了母语，整个教育方法和气氛都不健康。

终其一生他对学术的态度复杂，在孟加拉国，他鼓励头脑聪明的人从事各种学术领域，但他看不起大多数印度学者。1936年，他在桑提尼克坦说："我国有很多平庸者爬到学术成功的巅峰。"

在读到一本有关英国和中国鸦片交易的书之后，泰戈尔对英国向中国贩卖鸦片的行为充满愤怒。1916 年，在日本和美国的巡回演说中，他雄辩地提醒各国军国主义、民族主义、无节制的商业主义和为技术而技术的危险。在中国期间，他收到孙中山先生请求会晤的函件，在紫禁城里他见了退位的末代皇帝溥仪，甚至劝说军阀放下武器。活泼可爱的翻译林徽因给他留下深刻的印象，像一只色彩斑斓的小鸟在诗人身旁飞来飞去。然而，他的演说受到反对，第二次演讲结束离开演讲厅时，泰戈尔注意到一张中文传单，后来他得知中国激进派对他的贵族气质和温和的民主改革有微词。

在中国、日本和印度，他和这些国家的民族主义情绪不合拍，终于放弃了亚洲是一体的幻想。他还受邀访问了阿根廷、苏联、墨索里尼的意大利。

自 1878 年留学英国开始，泰戈尔的足迹踏至欧亚美非四大洲。获得诺贝尔奖后至 1931 年间，他曾多次访问英国、美国、德国、法国等，并两次访问中国，每到一处，都发表演说。他以开放自由的姿态看待西方文明，但同时对物质文明背后的精神危机深感忧虑。

纵观泰戈尔的生平事迹，他对民族前途和世界未来的担忧，以及对信仰的坚守，此中的爱、孤独、彷徨与挣扎等，在《吉檀迦利》中都有所体现。

1941 年 8 月 7 日，在北加尔各答他诞生的房子，泰戈尔的生命走到了终点。临终前几日，他写道：

我的前方是和平之海，

舵手，开船吧，

现在你是我的日常伙伴，

把我抱到你的膝上吧。

在我们通往无限的旅途中，

北极星独自闪现。

自由的赐予者，

给我自由吧。

愿你的宽恕和慈爱

成为我行程的永恒资粮，

愿凡俗的瓜葛了断，

愿广阔的宇宙拥抱我，

带着一颗勇敢的心，

愿我得以认识那伟大的不可知。

萧兴政

厦门大学外文学院英文系

2005 年初稿，2019 年春修订

作者简介

泰戈尔（Rabindranath Tagore）

1861年5月7日—1941年8月7日

印度诗人、文学家、哲学家，亚洲首位诺贝尔文学奖获奖者。他出身贵族，精通文学、音乐、绘画等，从小濡染印度宗教经典。青年时留学西方，汲取了西方的人文精神和科学精神，是一位具有宇宙意识的人道主义者。他的诗歌富有韵律美，充满自然的意象，散发着浓郁的抒情气息和哲思。1913年，泰戈尔因《吉檀迦利》获诺贝尔文学奖。另有著名诗集《新月集》《飞鸟集》等。

泰戈尔的诗直接影响了中国20世纪的新诗运动以及叶芝、庞德等西方诗人。他一生写了五十多部诗集，被尊为“诗圣”，在世界文坛具有重要地位。

译者简介

萧兴政

中英双语诗人，英文笔名X. Z. Shao，1964年生于福建省宁德市周宁县。执教于厦门大学外文学院英文系，主讲《英文诗歌阅读与创作》和《新闻英语听力》等课程。多次在剑桥大学出版社刊物English Today上发表英文诗歌、散文和论文。

2004年，翻译了《吉檀迦利》和《印度悲情曲》。2018年于台湾出版中文诗集《幽谷迷思》。近期，翻译完成纪伯伦的《先知》。

画家简介

马克 · 麦金尼斯（Mark W. McGinnis）

美国艺术家、作家，生于 1950 年 9 月，在南达科他州阿伯丁北方州立大学担任美术教授长达三十年。现住爱达荷州的博伊西。其艺术创作跨越多个领域，包括绘画、雕塑、影像等；此外，他还以研究为导向，创作了对不同主题进行探索的作品，包括物种灭绝，印度和日本的文学，科学与哲学等。

2001 年始，他围绕《吉檀迦利》的 103 首诗创作了 103 幅精美画作，荣获盛赞。

关于《吉檀迦利》系列插画

2001 年夏天，我开始阅读泰戈尔的著作，不久就发现了这部诗集《吉檀迦利》。我立刻觉得，我必须放下一切，去创作受这些诗歌启发的绘画。这部诗集共 103 首诗或“献歌”（孟加拉语：gitanjali）。我计划为每一首诗画一幅 23cm × 23cm 的画。我决定用较小的尺寸，以配合这些亲切细腻的诗作，这也暗合了几个世纪以来印度小幅画的传统。

为了创作《吉檀迦利》系列插图，我尽量把自己沉浸在泰戈尔的世界里。我阅读了他极具多元化和创造性的创作生涯中各个领域的作品：诗歌、散文、小说和书信等。这些画并不试图对诗歌做图解，而是由诗歌本身启发，以及我对泰戈尔富于创造力的心灵的理解而创作出的图象。这种理解也与我当时的审美观念以及不断翻衍变更的绘画技巧相融合。从一开始，我就决定这个创作计划不受单一风格的限制，而是，跟随每首诗对我灵感的激发，自由创作。这也使得这一系列的创作成为我极有价值的经历。

在这些画中，我倾向于使用较浓烈的色彩，这也与印度小幅画的传统相契合。画的边框也与这种传统有关，在我以往的创作中，我也常使用边框。在设计每幅画的边框时，我选择画作中的某些元素，并将它们设计成一种图案。为了区分边框和边框中画的内容，我特意选用了金属色的颜料用在边框上。我经过反复诵读《吉檀迦利》，并创作了诸多草图以尝试用不同的方式去表达这些诗，才最终使画的内容渐渐形成。在几幅画中，我用了非常个人化的表达，偶尔我通过“抽象”（abstraction）而非“表现”（representation）的方式加以表达。

泰戈尔的诗歌使我深受感动的是美丽的赤诚，这种赤诚，展现在他对永恒的探索，以及极力探寻自己和灵性世界的关系中。当他的诗中出现传统的奉爱意象的隐喻时，泰戈尔和他的印度宗教之源的联系就极为明显。在几幅画中，我用蓝色皮肤的形象暗指毗湿奴和他的一些化身，比如，克里希那，罗摩和佛陀等，以表达这种联系。然而，尽管我对印度宗教和文化有兴趣，可这并不是吸引我进入泰戈尔诗歌的主要因素。吸引我的东西是他的“普世性”（universality）。我相信，不论哪一种宗教追随者，或者不信教的人，都能从泰戈尔的智慧和洞见中得到启发。要创作与有如此深度的诗歌相配的视觉艺术作品，我感到有些力不从心。我希望我的画有助于吸引更多人去了解这位诗人的著作，我认为他是十九世纪晚期和二十世纪早期最伟大的智者之一。

马克·麦金尼斯（Mark W. McGinnis）

2019 年 7 月

吉檀迦利

作者 _ [印] 泰戈尔　译者 _ 萧兴政

产品经理 _ 牛长红　装帧设计 _ 王易　产品总监 _ 应凡　技术编辑 _ 刘世乐
责任印制 _ 梁拥军　出品人 _ 于桐

果麦
www.guomai.cc

以 微 小 的 力 量 推 动 文 明